Unlucky
TERROR

Unlucky TERROR

E. Charles Grant

Pen Culture Solutions
1-888-727-7204 (USA)
1-800-950-458 (Australia)
support@penculturesolutions.com

PART 1

Chapter 1

THE BEGINNING

Alex emerged from the trees and overgrown bushes as if he was thrown from them. He fell to the grass at the edge of Lyons Park. Alex sat on his knees, looking across the park to the supermarket. "People," he whispered to himself. He looked down at his hands and began to weep. He cradled his hands in his arms. The arms were strong, and his hands were large. His fingers hung down from his hands toward the earth. They weren't broken or cut but hung without bones like meaty pieces of yarn.

Alex then heard a voice. It sounded as if the wind were whispering to him. He knew that voice, and it wasn't the wind. This was his greed, his destiny; this was going to happen. The voice whispered, "You played, you pay, and today you say 'go away'?"

Alex stood up and said, "I won't do it." He then staggered across the park. Alex made his way through the park and saw the playground swing begin to sway against the wind with no one in it. He knew his time was short.

Finally, he reached the curb of the street. He stood there thinking of his life and decisions. Taking a deep breath and pulling his sunglasses down with his thumbs, Alex quietly said, "Let me see my wife."

Alex looked across the street and called out, "Karen! Don't go there! Come back!" He jumped off the curb and ran across the street to no one.

1

As he ran, he called out, "Karen!" A semitruck driver looking up from his phone locked his brakes, but it was too late. Alex was instantly killed.

Families from the park and supermarket parking lot began to scream. Standing around what was left of Alex, people began to talk. "Maybe he was blind or lost," a lady said.

An old woman outside the circle of people suddenly stopped looking at the scene and slowly turned toward the park. She saw the swing going back and forth empty as if someone was in it. Confused, the old woman thought she heard singing, but from where? Is the wind singing? she thought. That was not the only strange thing about the singing. The song didn't fit time; it was too old even for the lady. The voice sounded sinister and joyful. She calmly turned back around, but she can still make out the song. "We're all alone. No chaperone can get our number. The world's in slumber. Let's misbehave. There's something wild about you, child, that's so contagious. Let's be outrageous. Let's misbehave."

Chapter 2

Found Glasses

Sitting in his car, Michael looked across the parking lot into the intersection. He saw the McDonald's on the south side of the street. He saw the happy families sitting inside, and he remembered when his family was like that—his boy and his wife, now ex, consuming Mickey D's and loving life. Or so he thought. Just twenty minutes ago, he dropped his boy off at his ex's place. She didn't hate him; they just "grew apart."

"Well, what's for dinner? Fast food or good food?" he said to himself. He glanced at the grocery store to his right. Well, I used your parking lot to exchange my boy. Might as well buy your products.

He got out and walked into the store, where he tried to just buy what he needed. Impulse buyer . . . guilty. Chicken and veggies. While his boy was home, it was pizza and burgers. Not the greatest, but that's the kinda dad I am, he thought. He went to the checkout lanes, and only one register was open. Two people were ahead of him. Of course, one was a lady who was a thousand years old. She wanted to argue about every one of her items. He stood there quiet and patient.

For what seemed like an hour, he got through the lines. He pushed his cart to his car. He placed his groceries into his trunk and walked to the side of his car. He went to put his keys into his car, and something on the ground caught his eyes—sunglasses.

They looked like his old Oaks, but he knew they were not Oaks. They looked like someone dropped them right by his door. He looked around and then picked them up—no scratches just black sunglasses. He thought, This is lucky. Three days ago, he broke his worn-out old glasses. They just seemed to jump out of his hands and break in half. Ever since, he'd been squinting at the sun.

He said to the glasses, "From one guy, discarded, to another. Thanks, buddy." He got into his car and put on the glasses.

Gold, everything was gold. Just as soon as he put on the glasses, he pulled them off. What was that? he thought. Everything was gold. He slowly put the glasses back on. What he saw was gold—gold everywhere. It was as if the whole world were painted gold—light gold, dark gold, and every degree in between.

He didn't understand what he was seeing. He thought, How is this possible? The sky was a light gold, almost clear. The sun looked like a gold plate hanging in the sky. All around were dark gold trees and cars. The streets were lighter with gold grease spots on them.

"This is amazing," he said to himself.

He saw a golden couple cross in front of his car. He heard the lady say, "What do we need for dinner tonight?"

The man said, "I don't know."

She looked at him, and he can her say, You're such a help. But her mouth didn't move.

Did I just read her mind? Well, you're looking at a golden world. What's impossible? He chuckled to himself. He then looked at the lady and said, "Don't forget the wine."

The lady immediately said to the man, "Oh yeah, don't forget the wine."

He thought, Did I do that?

He then said, "And the dog food."

The lady said, "And we're out of dog food."

The man replied, "That's because we don't have a dog. Are you all right?"

She said, confused, "Yes. I don't know why I said that."

"Can I control minds?" Michael whispered to himself. Casino . . . casino. I can play cards and make lots of cash. But it may not work in a casino. Well, let's try. He put the glasses on the seat beside him and drove to the casino, forgetting about the groceries he had in his car.

He pulled up to the parking lot at the casino and felt weird. He always felt a little weird going to the casino during the day, almost like he was breaking an unspoken law. If you're not rich, under fifty-five, and broke, don't come in. If you do, you're a degenerate gambler. Well, he'd been called worse. He strolled in.

As he walked in, his senses were overwhelmed with lights and bells. After going through security, he put on his glasses. The casino immediately turned different shades of gold. He looked around; he noticed something strange. Different machines were glowing levels of gold as if one machine was at sixty watts and another at one hundred. He thought, Could it be that easy?

He sat at a machine glowing one hundred watts of gold. Michael fed a $20 bill and played max bet. After a few pulls of the lever, bells went off—$1,000. He yelled out, "Wooo!" He looked around and saw other machines glow. Some got brighter as others got dimmer. He continued to play machines, winning $5,000 in total.

He went to the casino restaurant and treated himself to a steak dinner. As Michael ate, he thought of all the possibilities he can do with his newfound treasure. He thought, OK, these are special glasses. Someone made these, so either they lost them or someone is watching me. Maybe all this is a test. I'll wait awhile until I use them. I won't use them to pick up women, just in case someone is watching. I'll wait a week and think about what I should do. So Michael headed home from the casino, thinking about all the possibilities.

The next week, Michael decided to not use the glasses. He thought that either they were supernatural and maybe dangerous or someone created them, and this was a test. Michael went to the library to research myths and other things. It was difficult because of the renovations at the main branch. He decided to return when it was complete. The library was adding a new local history wing.

At home, Michael sat in his favorite chair with the glasses in hand. "OK, maybe these can work like Siri," Michael said to himself. He took a long breath and put on the glasses. It was the same golden world he remembered. This time, he spoke to the glasses. "OK, glasses. Do you have rules? Do you have a guide I can speak with? Am I amiss in using you?" Michael sat for a second, hoping nothing would happen. He was about to take off the glasses when he noticed it.

A small wooden door appeared on his wall. It was about two feet tall with a rounded top. He stared at the door and noticed that it turned from gold to dark brown with iron braces across the middle. A bright glow came from cracks in the door and from around the frame. The rest of his room changed from gold to the natural colors. His golden world was gone. In his mind, Michael grew nervous. He knew he did something to change the game. If it was good or bad, he would find out soon.

His room began to brighten as the small door slowly opened. A small person emerged from the door. He looked like a leprechaun but not dressed in green. There were no shamrocks in his hat or golden buckles on his shoes. The little man had a beard with no mustache. His jacket was dark brown with a matching vest under it. He looked around the room until his deep blue eyes fixed on Michael. The little man said with an Irish accent, "Hello, Michael."

Michael instantly said, "Are you a leprechaun?"

The little man began to laugh. He walked over to a stack of books on the floor and sat on them like a chair. "Well, yes and no. I am from an ancient people. Myths, legends, and stories change. A pot of gold—the first gifts we gave your people was a pot of knowledge. Your people started calling it treasure. The treasure turned into gold," the little man said.

Michael looked at him, stunned.

"My name is Patrick. I changed it about five hundred years ago. I am the guide you asked for. Most people don't ask for help. They just take their money and end up losing," Patrick said with a disappointed look on his face.

"Losing?" Michael muttered.

Patrick started, "I'm getting ahead of myself. Those glasses you found are just one of many gifts we give people to test you. It is a wager between us and the dark set of my people. Many centuries ago, my grandfather was saved by one of your people. A wolf was going to eat him when a young boy used a sling to slay the beast. They became friends. The boy was given a pot. This pot would reveal different truths to him when it was filled with water. It told him the future, past, magic, and different treasures. The boy helped many people, and their friendship grew. Our people began to trust your people. Of course, a human would mess that up.

"One of the leaders of my people named Milcom came across a man sleeping by an old tree. He didn't disturb the man. He just walked on the path. What Milcom didn't realize was that the man was waiting for one of us. Milcom fell into his trap. The greedy man held him and forced him to give him treasure. 'Give me your pot of gold,' he told him. Milcom tricked the man out of his soul. Ever since then, Milcom and his followers try to trick people from their souls.

"My grandfather didn't stand for this. He couldn't defeat Milcom, and he didn't want his people to suffer from a war. So a wager was made between my people. Two tokens are given to two of your people per generation. These tokens will allow the receivers to have many gifts. Now these tokens also send the recipients on very dangerous quests. You must do some good, defeat some evil, and stop your counterpart. Your counterpart must do evil that causes terror in a good person, defeat a good person who will try to stop your counterpart, and stop you. A red moon will signal the battle between the two of you. You will fight for the right to influence people."

"Are you nuts? I'm not fighting anyone! Take this back!" Michael shouted at him.

"Too late. You already used them. If you give up, try to run, you'll die. If you die, the greedy person will receive the prize. That's OK, they've won more times than I can remember. I guess your people could survive another Jim Jones, H. H. Holmes, or Martin Dumollard. Now Hitler is a different story. His occult society found Milcom. Heinrich Himmler was actually Milcom's man. He unleashed a demon into old Adolf and couldn't control it. Just because someone wins the prize doesn't mean they are invincible. Plus, Heinrich was kind of dumb. You can see our glasses in his last picture. Back to my instructions, all you have to do is ask the glasses to show you people to help, missing people, or give the name of people you wish to help. Be careful, you won't like what you see."

Michael just sat there, helpless. Patrick smiled and said, "Milcom has chosen his person. He will show him a part of your journey. You get to see him and a piece of his journey. Your counterpart has already begun. Beware of him, for he is evil. I will try to show you a weakness of his." Michael nodded and agreed to see.

Michael instantly saw himself sitting at the park. It was like he was watching a movie with VR glasses where he was the star. He watched himself sit on a bench. Michael was confused about what he saw. In the park, on a swing, was a dirty little man. Michael thought he looked like Patrick, but his skin was pitch black. His suit was black and dirty. The little man's hair was long and oily. The eyes were what startled Michael. His eyes glowed a bright yellow. They reflected like a wolf's eyes when you shone light into them. The little man rocked back and forth, not taking his eyes off Michael. Michael can smell him. He didn't know how, but he can smell him. He smelled like a mixture of human waste, mildew, and sulfur.

The little man began to sing to Michael, "On the good ship Lollipop, it's a sweet trip to a candy shop, where bonbons play on the sunny beach of Peppermint Bay . . . hey, hey."

Michael looked away in disgust. He looked back, and the little man was gone from the swing. He instantly saw and smelled the little man sitting next to him on the bench.

"Hello, Michael," the little man said.

Michael was frozen with terror.

"I do believe you know who I am. Welcome to the end of your life. I will give you a free pass out of this journey. All I need from you is your eyes." Milcom pulled out a wooden spoon. "I'll just scoop them out, and you'll be free." Milcom smiled. "Well, I guess I'll take that as a no.

In accordance with the wager, you get to see my boyo in action. He's already ahead of you. Don't worry, you won't face him." Milcom began to laugh uncontrollably. "Sorry, you'll get that joke later. One of my other friends will handle you."

Milcom jumped off the bench and skipped toward the merry-go-round. He jumped on with kids already playing on it. They can't see him, but their faces changed to a scowl as if they can smell him. He jumped off and disappeared into the bushes on the edge of the park.

Michael was still afraid, and confusion ran through his mind. The glasses went dark, and he can't see a thing. He heard something moving in the dark—no, something swinging in the dark.

Chapter 3

Hanging Jenni

Jenni woke and slowly opened her eyes. She didn't see anything. The room was pitch black, and the smell was musty. It was like whoever built this room was growing mold on purpose. She felt a sharp pain from her wrist. She was hanging by them. She thought, How did I get here? What was the last thing she could remember? She was sitting in her car, and then someone was behind her. In the car? Yes, someone was behind her. Just then, a blinding light came on. A basement, I'm hanging in a dirty, windowless basement.

She looked down and saw a small square piece of wood. She stood on it to give her wrists a break. The walls of the basement were earth just as the floor. She looked around and saw an old wooden table with a typewriter on it. The typewriter was very old. She can make out "Remington" on the back, but some letters were worn off. A chair was behind the typewriter. To her right was an old army duffel bag. The bag was full and hanging on a hook. The bottom of the bag was stained; it looked like tar. She thought, Is that oil or . . . blood? She wanted to scream, but she can't.

A door creaked open, and a figure walked around her with a briefcase in their hands. The person put the briefcase beside the typewriter and opened it. They pulled paper out of it and loaded it into the typewriter. She knew she was in trouble and thought, This person is crazy.

"Hello, Jen," she heard the person say.

She thought, It's a man . . . a crazy fucking man. He was dressed in an old suit. He was wearing a full-body black suit, the kind made of spandex. She saw similar suits on TV. She was watching basketball with her friends when a kid wore in his team's colors a suit like that. You couldn't see the kid's face, only the suit. That was kind of creepy, but this guy had a mask over his face. The mask looked like a mannequin's face that had been cut off the mannequin's head. To finish it off, he wore a pair of black sunglasses.

"I said hello, Jen. Now don't be rude," the man said.

"Please let me go. I won't tell on you. I can't even see who you are. Please!" Jenni cried out.

"Now, Jen, let's not start that. I know you have no idea who I am. I've been watching you a long time. You are a good person. You are an interesting person. So . . . you are going to tell me a story. A story is what I need. You tell me a good original story, you'll wake up far from here. We will never meet again—well, unless you want to see me again." He chuckled to himself. "So, Jen, if you don't help me, you'll end up like Nick over there. Yes, yes, that lump in the bag was Nick. I'm an equal opportunity psychopath. Nick had no stories—well, kind of. He could only tell me movies. So he failed, I tortured him, I placed him into the bag, and there he hangs. He was alive when he was hung upside down in the bag. He lasted a few days. I suspect that you will last longer. I mean, you do spin classes." He chuckled to himself again.

He sat down behind the typewriter and didn't make a sound. Jenni can't see his hands. All she can see was the typewriter to his shoulders and that blank mannequin's face with the sunglasses. She thought those glasses must cover holes to his eyes. The typewriter started working, and the man laughed to himself. She thought, A story . . . a story . . . I'm scared shitless. The end. The typewriter kept going.

He laughed and said, "OK, Jen, I know you're scared. So I'll tell you a story. That's only fair. I told Nick one, but I don't think he really listened. Will you listen, Jen, or will you wait for your turn to speak?"

Jen took a deep breath and said, "Yes, I'll listen, s-s-s-sir."

The man replied, "Sir? No, no, no, the man I murdered for this suit was a sir. I'm so rude. Let me introduce myself. My name is E. Charles Grant. Now I go by E. and not Edward because I'll never live up to my father. He was an Edward. I'm just an E. I was born in a midwestern city by two loving parents. I went to Catholic school. I played Nintendo and sports. I respected the rules of society. I used to work at a shopping mall as a young man, a department store in the mall. I was a stock boy. I worked there. I became jealous. I was not jealous of the high school quarterback or the cheerleader/cashier. No, I was jealous of the mannequin whose face I don before you. Every day I would work, this idol to fashion would mock me. He stood there wearing the latest fashion. He had a perfect body and stood above everyone that would walk by. People notice him. They respected him. I think they would have invited him over for dinner. The mere presence of him made people buy clothes. So one day I replaced him with another of his kind. I took him home. Of course, no one noticed I did this. He has been mine ever since."

Mr. Grant spoke, and the typewriter never stopped. He began to speak again. "So my life putters along with no major events happening until . . . I found these glasses. I was under a bridge. I won't say where, but it's by a creek, a very shallow creek. So I was sitting under my bridge when a man landed face-first into the shallow creek bed. I went over to him to see his lifeless body. When I saw him, these glasses were what was left on his face. The glasses should be destroyed, but they aren't. I mean, his head looked like a smashed pumpkin . . . zero, right, but they are perfect. I put them on, and I saw . . . I saw . . . I saw . . . I saw new.

"Later in my journey with my new glasses, I stumbled into an old knickknack store. This typewriter glowed for me. The old man who sold it to me was hesitant, but he knew I was determined to buy it. When I got home and loaded the paper, it spoke to me. Now I don't know, but it started talking. I mean, it started typing to me. I asked it to tell me its story. Are you still with me, Jen?" he whispered.

Jenni slowly nodded.

"Good!" he exclaimed. "Now this a Remington typewriter built in 1923. The original owner was a Steven Jones . . . pretty common name. He had it for some time until he shipped it to some family member in the old country—Warsaw, I believe. I know what you're thinking, Jen, and you're right. It was seized by the Nazi invaders. It was then used at Treblinka to catalog many unfortunate souls. So somehow all that hate bled into this typewriter. All the typewriter asks is to be given stories. I give it stories, and the black spot stays away. He scanned the room and looked back at Jenni.

She thought, OK, OK, tell him a story, and you may survive this. My mouth is so dry. That's all I can think about.

The man said, "Now if you're thirsty, I can offer you a drink. It's hose water. It's not laced with anything, so don't freak out."

She nodded. A stream of water appeared in front of her. A hose above her poured water just in front of her face. She hesitated but thought, Might as well. After her drink, she took a deep breath and calmed down.

"OK, a story," she said.

"Jen, I wasn't completely honest with you. The man on the bridge—well, I pushed him off it. Something whispered to me to take the glasses. No one saw me do it, but I liked it—the thrill of almost being caught," Mr. Grant said.

Jenni thought, Story . . . story, how can I think of a story as long as he keeps typing? I mean, he's typing now. I haven't said shit. A story . . . a story . . . a story to save my life . . . Jason!

She remembered a story her friend Jason told her years ago. He told her, "Jen, this story may save your life."

She thought, Well, Jason, it didn't get you second base with me, but I hope it saves my life.

Jenni started, "OK, this is a story my friend told me. His name is Jason, and he's Native American. He's not full blooded, but his grandfather is . . . I think. He said that this story came from his grandfather who heard it from his grandfather, back many generations. The nations did not settle in certain areas of America because of tree demons. Now he said the actual name, but I can't remember how to pronounce it.

"The legend goes these demons lived in the forest. They feed on people and their fear. The demon would appear in the early mornings, after most people went to sleep but before the sunrise. They would feed on their souls and turn the victims into twisted trees along bodies of water. The way they stopped the demons or, I guess, contained them was to imprison them. They made ruin stones—stones that had old images of powerful gods on them. They sacrificed things, animals, and enemies on these stones. They would locate these demons and wait for the day. In the daytime, the demons were trees. During the night hours, they would feed. There are still many ruins around the US with demons trapped inside. He also said that lots of monsters, like you, are because of these demons. Because of deforestation, many demons were burned and released into the air in spirit form while others were built into houses, axes, rifles, and even books. So he said to stay away from forest parks at night, especially the parks with old rocks—ruins—around them."

The typing stopped, and the man slowly shook his head. "Jen, Jen, Jen, it seems like Jason just may have saved your life. That was the best story I've heard so far."

The typing began again, and she thought, This guy is a liar. He's still typing. I'm going to die.

The man slowly stood up and walked over to a small cabinet door hanging on the wall. The door had two strips of tape on it with names on each of them. Jenni thought, What is he doing? What names are on there? Elaine and . . . oh my god! The typewriter is still typing. It stops every time I stop . . . thinking? That can't be possible. What's he writing?

The man wrote "Jen and the Tree Demons." "There, Jen, all done. You have earned your freedom. Well, I guess Jason has. You might let him get to second base with you." Jenni then realized that she didn't say that. She only thought that.

He walked over to Jenni and stood a foot in front of her face. "Goodbye, Jen. I'll be in touch." The man slowly grabbed the side of his glasses with one hand and removed them. Jenni was in complete terror. She saw no eyes. The mannequin's face was not cut with eye holes.

Before she can scream, a sharp pain hit her shoulder. A needle, she thought as she slowly fell asleep.

Jenni felt a person shaking her shoulder. She realized that she was on a bench in the park two blocks from her house. An old woman walking her dog was talking to her. "Honey, are you OK? I see your wrists are hurt. I called the police. It's going to be OK."

Jenni was still dazed. "How long have I been here?" she said in a scratchy voice.

"Well, Boomer and I just got here. I saw you lying there, and I thought you looked like that missing girl," the old woman said.

"I was taken," Jenni said.

The old woman gave a concerned look and said, "Honey, why don't you tell me your story?"

Jenni began to scream as the police sirens closed in.

Chapter 4

THE COUNTY PARK

Michael put his hands on his face and began to cry. Patrick was standing in the doorway to his little world. "I'm sorry, Michael. Try tomorrow, and you'll do fine. I'll check in with you after the new moon. Try to help the young and old. When you're feeling up to it, try to give mercy to someone who doesn't know they are getting mercy." Patrick closed the door behind him, and the door faded away.

Michael took off his glasses and went to bed. He left the lights on in his room and the hallway. Michael woke up the next day praying last night was a nightmare but knowing it wasn't. He sat looking at the TV. He thought, What do I do? And the TV gave him an idea.

"Two local teens went missing last week," the reporter said.

Michael put on the glasses and said, "Tell me what happened to those kids."

The night was cool, calm, and a little cold as four teenagers sat at the county park. They were at a shelter that no one ever used. Jake took a long drink out of a bottle wrapped in a brown paper bag. He passed the bottle to Jim and said, "That's sweet, buddy. Take a drag and pass it on."

Jim took a swig and passed it to his girlfriend, Sara. Sara and Jim had been dating since freshman year. She loved him but worried that they wouldn't last. She was accepted to K State, and Jim wasn't. Jim would probably learn a trade if he was lucky. He worked at the local pizza restaurant.

Sara took a small drink and then passed the bottle to Kim. Kim took a long drag off her cigarette and then took her drink. Kim and Jake had been dating for a year. She liked her "bad boy" but also realized that she'd leave with Sara this fall for school.

The bottle made two circles around the group. Jake took a hard long drag off his cigarette and said, "Every anticigarette commercial makes me wanna smoke more." The group laughed and looked at one another.

Jim said to Jake, "Tell a ghost story like you used to do. Come on, man."

Jake smiled and nodded. He took another drag off his smoke and began his story. "OK, this is our spot. Jim and I have been coming here since we were kids. The park closes at midnight, but that doesn't matter to us. About twenty years ago, this park was open twenty-four hours a day. You could camp out here, and it was cool. Back in the day, this park was busy as hell. Local day-care centers would come here and play in the park."

Jake took a drink and passed the bottle. He continued, "Warrick Hospital also came out here."

Kim said, "That's a mental institution, isn't it?"

Jake smiled and said, "Yes, it is, sugar, a crazy house for the criminally insane. They would bring nonviolent patients here for therapy. One day they brought some patients to the park. It was the same day as a day care was out here. The guys watching the patients kept them away from the kids. As the day went on, the dudes watching the patients started talking to the hot day-care ladies."

Kim looked at Jake with a disapproving glance. Jake said, "Not as hot as you, baby. So the crazies started intermingling with the kids.

This continued for a while until the boss of the day care showed up and started shouting at them, telling them to get those crazy guys away from her kids. The kids and patients were broken up. They did a head count. They were missing five patients. The dudes watching the patients knew they would get fired or even go to the slammer for this fuckup. They changed the paperwork to show that those guys never came to the park. So days later, the news put out that they had escaped mental patients, but nobody paid attention.

"My uncle T. used to be a park ranger here. He's retired now in Texas. He told me that rangers used to drink up in shelters after dark. That's one of the reasons we come out here. Nobody messes with us because the park is closed. Rangers now just close the gates and crash out at the ranger cabin.

"So a couple of weeks later, some rangers are having a party up here, the campsite over there by the lake. One of the rangers who was working the late shift came by before midnight and hung out with his buddies. He told them to save some beers for him, and he would be back after he did one last round. The ranger did his round and headed back to the campsite. He returned, and the site was all messed up. Chairs and coolers were knocked over. The fire looked as if someone was thrown into it. He thought his buddies were messing with him. He saw one of his buddies lying on the ground face-first. The ranger walked over to him and told him to get up. The guy didn't move, so the ranger pulled him over to his back. That guy's face was ripped off."

Both girls screamed out in terror. Jim smiled and said, "Awesome."

Jake continued, "So there was a huge manhunt. Now if you look on the internet, you won't see the manhunt because they wanted to keep it low key. I guess one of the guards was the mayor or governor's kid, and they would get in trouble. If you look it online, there was a renovation. No one was found. They started closing the park at midnight for safety."

Kim said, "Whatever, that's not true."

Jake finished off the bottle and said, "Oh yes, it is. Every once in a while, you'll hear a ranger or a fisherman say they saw a guy running through the woods in dirty white clothes, white outfits like they have at Warrick."

A large bang exploded, and they all screamed out. Jake had pulled out the bottle from the paper bag and smashed it with his hands. Sara shouted, "You asshole!" Jake smiled at them with delight.

The two boys walked over to the edge of the shelter clearing and began to pee. Jake threw the empty bottle into the woods before he began. The girls shouted out, "What's that?"

Jim called out, "It's the crazies in the woods!" The boys began to laugh as they walked back. They stood around joking and smoking their cigarettes.

They heard a rustle in the woods. Sara said, "What's that?"

Jake knew that if Sara was scared, he wouldn't be getting any action tonight. "It's the woods. There are animals out there, and I just threw a bottle. We can go, OK?"

Sara asked, "What time is it?"

Kim replied, "Three a.m."

Jim said to the group, "There is something big out there."

Jake said, "Dude, don't. The girls are already scared."

Jim replied, "No, seriously, can you hear that? Look at the trees." The group looked at the trees and saw them moving beyond what the wind was doing to them. They also heard branches snapping and wood creaking. The kids stood frozen with fear and awe behind their car. The trees seemed to move as if a creature as large as a tree was moving them. They can't see too clearly because the shelter area was not very well lit. There was only one streetlight by the shelter.

Whatever was moving came closer. Finally, two slender trees about five feet apart were pushed away from each other into a large V. A slender, treelike creature emerged from the dark woods. The creature was over two stories tall. This creature's body looked like tree bark. Sara could only produce a small wimpier. Its arms and legs reminded her of a giant daddy longlegs. Its head looked like a wooden praying mantis with two long horns. Jim whispered, "The eyes." The eyes looked like a wolf's eyes glowing in the night.

It stood before them and spoke with a creaky, whiny voice. Welcome. I see you have decided to grace us with your presence. I am the one who has no name. I am the keeper of these trees . . . kept. I am the prisoner of this forest. So I take prisoners, said the creature. The kids can hear the creature, but its mouth wasn't moving. It was speaking to them with its mind.

It insidiously said, The people trapped me here with their little pebbles. They left me here alone. The people were driven off by your people. Your people don't care about our prisons. So I keep your people. I trap your souls by my lake. Those trees that look like tortured souls, they are my tortured souls. The creature crouched down, and its mouth opened. Its mouth was layered with teeth like a shark's, but they were wooden stakes the size of long screwdrivers.

Kim suddenly broke free from their trance. She screamed, "Let's get the fuck out of here!" The kids suddenly ran to their car. They jumped in, and Jake started it up. Both girls looked out the back window and saw the creature running toward them like a giant wooden spider. Jake pulled off, almost crashing into a tree. The kids raced down the winding road with the creature running behind. They flew over a turtle bridge that led to the kid's park and entrance. The girls saw the creature stop by the bridge, but they noticed it didn't cross.

Jake drove to the nearest gas station, where the kids talked. Jim and Kim wanted to call the cops or the rangers. Jake and Sara wanted to go home and forget this ever happened. Jim said, "I'm going to the ranger's office tomorrow." Kim agreed and said she was going with him.

Jake shouted, "Go ahead and get eaten by that monster!"

Kim said, "No, wait, it didn't cross the bridge. Maybe it's trapped behind the bridge. Daytime, we'll go during the day. That way, people will be there."

Jake whispered, "Go I'm not."

The next day, Jim picked up Kim, and they headed to the ranger's office. Jim called the office and asked to speak with a ranger in person. They drove down an isolated road toward the park's entrance. Both kids felt like they were returning to the scene of a crime. Approaching the entrance, Kim told Jim to pull over. They stopped by the caretaker's cabin, which was outside the park. It was an old cabin with a prefab house next to it. "Look, Jim," Kim said. The kids walked up to two stone slabs on each side of the entrance to the park. The stones were sticking out of the ground like Stonehenge. Both stone had carvings in them, and they looked very old. Kim pulled her phone out and took pictures of them.

"They are old," a voice said from behind the kids.

They turned around quickly. "Mr. Blackfoot, it's you," Jim said with relief.

"Yes, Jim. How's your dad?"

Jim told him that his dad was OK, but he wanted to know about the stones. Mr. Blackfoot said, "These stones were left by the native people of this land. They surround the entire park. That's over four hundred acres with a stone every hundred yards."

Kim said, "Have you ever seen anything weird out here at night?"

"No, young lady, because I don't go inside the park at night. Neither should you, kids," Mr. Blackfoot said.

Jim replied, "Well, we have a meeting at the ranger's office." Both kids got back in the car and drove to the office. They approached the office, and Kim looked at the bridge. She looked at the last place she saw the creature, and a cold shiver went down her spine. They pulled into the parking lot of the kid's area. Kids and parents were at the swings. Seeing the families made them at ease. The ranger's truck was parked out front.

Both kids walked into the office and saw a ranger with his feet up, watching TV. "Can I help you?" the ranger said. He was a slender older man. Most of the rangers were retired police officers. His hair was gray, and his eyes were light green. The man's face was worn, but he had a strong jaw.

Jim started, "Yes, we have a story to tell you." He told the story to the ranger. He didn't leave out the drinking, thinking that if he lied about one thing, they wouldn't believe the whole thing.

The ranger smiled and said, "You really want me to believe this?"

Kim said, almost begging, "Yes, it happened like that. Please believe us."

"I think you kids should go home and forget what you think you saw," the ranger said while turning back to the TV.

Kim then uttered, "Well then, we'll just put it on social media. I'm sure some ghost hunters will come out for this. Maybe some internet debunkers will sneak out here."

The ranger picked up the remote and turned off the TV. He didn't look at them. The kids just stared at the man as he blankly watched at the TV. A crackle of lightning struck across the sky. The kids can see it through the window facing the park. They realized the families had all left, and they were alone with the ranger in the park. Jim turned around and saw that the ranger's truck looked different. He saw that the driver's side was missing both tires, and it was being held up by cinder blocks.

The ranger slowly stood up, but as he stood, he didn't stop. He seemed to grow like a tree. The ranger slowly morphed into their nightmare. Instantly, they were standing in front of the tree monster as the skies opened up with rain. Because of the rain and lightning, if there was anyone around, their screams could not be heard.

"Thank you for tuning in with us tonight. The search for two local teens at the county park. Law enforcement officials stated that the male party's vehicle was located at the ranger's station. It was unknown if the kids entered the station. They don't believe they did because it was locked. Any tips, please call the hotline," the reporter said just as the ranger turned it off at the station.

Two park rangers slowly walked out of the station toward the kid's park by the lake. "So, Chris, what do you think happened?" said one to another.

"I think they were dating, and they didn't want their other boyfriend/girlfriend to know about it," said the ranger. Both men shrugged and looked at the lake. They stared at two trees by the lake. Both trees were twisted and looked as if they were attempting to claw their way off the bank.

"Good morning," the reporter said on the television. "The main branch of our public library will be getting a makeover. The library will have a local history wing. Pictures and artifacts from the city and county will be on display. They will even have ancient stones from the county lake. These stones have been removed and will be placed in the Native American section. Looking for a job? After thirty-five years, the county lake is looking for a new caretaker. The old caretaker will be retiring this spring."

Michael removed the glasses and sat there, stunned. "This is going to be hard," he said quietly to himself.

Chapter 5

Infinite Dollar

Michael tried to use the glasses as basic as he could. He would do small stuff and work up to harder questions. Missing kids might be too much for now. He went to the store and foresaw a lady leaving her purse. A ghostlike figure of the woman left her purse in a cart. Moments later, the real lady would appear. He was able to run her down and return her purse.

The next day, he foresaw a little boy get hit by a car, chasing after a ball. Michael stood where the ball would roll. When the ball came to him, he caught it and gave it back to the boy. The boy looked a little upset that he touched his ball. Michael just smiled and walked away.

A week of his good deeds had gone by, and Michael finally got the nerve to ask the glasses a harder question. He sat in his recliner and then Michael asked, "Let me show mercy to someone who won't see the mercy." The glasses went dark.

"New Orleans, baby!" three men shouted from their car. Driving down Highway 10, the men were tired of being in their rental car. This was their yearly trip somewhere. Last year, they went to Las Vegas. That was a great time. Vegas was always, but these guys had always talked about New Orleans.

John, Carl, and Joe had been friends since they were kids. They went to high school together. John and Carl went to college together. John finished, and Carl didn't. Joe went to work for his dad, who owned a car dealership.

The three men arrived at their hotel. It was an expensive hotel overlooking the French Quarter. Carl said, "When I make my millions, I'll come back and buy this place."

Joe laughed and said, "Man, I'll just settle for you picking up the tab." The men laughed and went inside. They got settled into their rooms and went to get dinner.

At dinner, the men had one too many. They started hassling their waitress. The men changed their minds about their orders. They gave the overworked lady a hard time. John asked for the tab. "Have a dollar day?" Carl asked. The other two men nodded and proceeded. For the men, "have a dollar day" meant that if they didn't like the service, they would leave a single dollar. John paid the $80 tab and left a dollar for a tip, which was pretty crappy.

The three drunk/buzzed men stumbled into a knickknack shop. The shop was run by an elderly Creole couple. "Welcome, boys," the lady said. The men waved and walked around the store.

Carl went up to the lady and said, "Where's the voodoo stuff?"

The lady pointed to the back and said, "Careful, honey, it ain't a board game."

Carl said with an arrogant tone, "This stuff is fake. Are you telling me a doll is going to change my life?" The men walked over to the dolls and started playing with them with utter contempt.

The lady put a red ruby to her eye and looked at the men through it. Through the ruby, she could see the true nature of their souls. She smiled and said, "Boys, you want real magic?"

The men started laughing and walked back to her. John said, "Sure, lady. What do you have for us?"

The lady smiled and said, "I have a special treat for you. It will cost you a dollar each. The good thing is that you'll get that dollar back in time." The men smiled and pulled out a dollar each. "Think about what you want most in the world—money, women, fame, or long life. Think about this, prick your finger, and squeeze blood onto these spoons."

John laughed again and said, "I'm just drunk enough to do this." He kept repeating the word wealthy. The lady pulled out a stick with an S carved out of the bottom like a stamp. She stamped the stick into his blood and then stamped his dollar.

Joe asked, "So what's that going to do?"

She replied, "After this happens, send your dollars into the world. When the dollar is gone, you'll begin to get wealthy. You'll be famous, or for you who wants to be strong and youthful, it will start. No more spare tire, only washboards and broad chest." She laughed. "When the dollar comes back, you lose these gifts." Joe instantly remembered that he had a Where's George dollar. He could track that dollar, so that was what he would use.

Carl started saying "fame" as he squeezed his blood. The process continued until Joe said, "Long life with youth."

The lady stopped and said, "Are you sure?" Joe nodded, and the process continued.

The lady said, "It is done. Have a nice day, boys. We are now closed."

The men laughed and walked out. Outside the store, they looked at one another. They looked back at the store, and they saw the reflection of the waitress smiling at them. The image faded, and all they saw were themselves looking at the shop. They went to a bar and bought three shots. The three dollars they sent as a tip. Joe was careful to snap a picture of the dollar to keep track online. The night went on as they drank it away.

The next morning, Joe got up before John and Carl. It was easy because they would sleep until noon. Joe walked back to the restaurant where they gave the poor tip. He asked the manager on duty if the waitress would be working today. He wanted to apologize to her for the hard time and lousy tip. The manager told him she was working the breakfast shift. The waitress instantly remembered him. Joe said, "I'm so sorry we were douchebags to you last night. We had way too much to drink, but that's no excuse. Please take this tip. If you don't want to keep it, please use it to buy someone's breakfast. I'm sorry."

The waitress said, "I'll take your tip and apology." Joe then smiled and left.

The waitress then looked into Michael's eyes, who was watching with his glasses in his chair. She said, "I hope mercy finds you." Michael instantly knew that she could see him. He took a deep breath and continued to watch this story.

John

After the trip, John returned home. He forgot about the dollar. He walked in, and his girlfriend was crying. John asked what was wrong. His girl told him that her father had died. He comforted her, and they went to her family's house. The funeral was beautiful. His girlfriend had one sister who hated him. John didn't care because he didn't like her either.

He didn't realize how much money they had. In her father's will, she got a beach house, stocks, and $2.3 million. With John's assistance, his girl turned the $2.3 million to $23 million. They planned to marry. At his bachelor party, a friend gave him a stack of one-dollar bills for the night. As he waited at the bar for the party bus and the rest of his friends to show, John fingered his way through the cash. His gaze fixed on one of the bills. It had an S, a red one. A few seconds passed, and then he remembered that night in New Orleans.

Carl and Joe walked into the bar. They noticed that John looked like he saw a ghost. They both asked what was wrong. John showed them the bill. Joe asked how he knew it was his bill. It could have been either one. Joe kept quiet about his bill. John said, "It's mine. I know it. I put a mustache on old George. Look, it's here with an S on it."

Carl laughed at John and said, "I guess you better marry that girl quick."

At that moment, John's phone rang. It was his girlfriend's best friend. She called to tell John to go to the hospital. His girlfriend was just in an accident. John's girlfriend would pass away from her injuries. With her wedding plans making her so busy, she forgot to change her last will. His girlfriend's sister, Jessica, was the sole heir to her estate. Jessica would make sure that John was as broke as the day he went to New Orleans.

Carl

Carl came home from his New Orleans trip and went straight to work. He was currently a half owner of a custom garage. He was the financial guy while the other owner was the mechanic. His partner told him that a major TV network wanted to do a series on them, the kind of series where they worked on cars. Carl's fame skyrocketed from local celebrity to national. He wasn't too famous not to attend his buddy's bachelor party. At this party was where the three men encountered the first of the dollars. John had lost his girlfriend and his soon-to-be fortune.

Joe had asked Carl if he marked his bill. He did. The mark he made was a joke toward Joe. Where it said "Washington, DC," Carl had put an arrow pointing up between the A and S. At the tip of the arrow was an R. Joe gave out an uneasy laugh and said, "Warshington." Even autocorrect knows it's wrong.

Carl returned home, and his partner asked to meet him at the local bar. His partner told him that the show was getting canceled. Carl was upset and told him that they would be okay. His partner told him that he was leaving the partnership and moving to Texas for a new show. Carl felt as if he was getting left. As his partner got up to leave, he put down some cash to pay for the tab. "Sorry, man, I got your drinks," his partner said. Carl sat at the bar staring at the dollar bill on top. "Warshington" was looking him in the face.

Joe

Joe had returned home from New Orleans and to work. He had noticed that his teeth were brighter. His face looked smooth and healthy. It was like he was airbrushed for a magazine. At work, Joe sold many more cars than before. He had many more dates with ladies who normally would not give him the time of day. When Joe saw what happened to John and Carl, he got scared. Youth and long life—when the dollar found him, would he turn old and die?

Joe looked up his dollar on Where's George. The dollar had been on a journey. He noticed that the dollar would travel round his hometown—Denver, Omaha, Iowa City, Saint Louis, and Oklahoma City. When he would go out of town, like Philadelphia, it was close to that city. This happened until John's girlfriend died. There were no more reports after that. He didn't know what to do. Joe didn't think about it much after that. He felt it would be a surprise.

Michael sat in his chair and watched the highlights of Joe's life with the glasses. Joe got married, had kids, took over his father's dealership, and had a pretty good life. Michael noticed that his family and friends got older, while he looked the same. The images seemed to get fuzzy as if he were looking into the future. Joe lost his parents and older friends. His wife grew old and died.

The glasses changed their images again. Michael seemed to be looking down a tunnel at Joe's life. He saw Joe bury his kids and his grandkids, and then the image changed again. Michael felt as if he was looking through binoculars backward. There was a tiny image of a young man looking at a lake. Some kind of drone dropped a package by him. Joe opened it and then dropped it. Dollar bills started floating from the open box. Joe looked heartbroken. Michael realized that Joe would look for that dollar for eternity and never find it. He would remain young for eternity. Only getting that dollar back would end his suffering in the future.

The image then faded to a clear picture of Michael's local bar. He walked down to the bar and had a drink. He thought, How do I help them? Michael paid his tab with a twenty. Michael looked at the change, and his mouth dropped open. Joe's dollar was in his hand.

Michael walked home and found an old Christmas card he never used. In the front, it said, "Life is a gift." Inside, the card said, "Enjoy yours." Michael asked the glasses for Joe's address and to show him what would happen after Michael mailed Joe the dollar. He saw Joe open the card. Joe began to cry as he held the dollar. "Thank you," Joe said as he lowered his head to the desk. He then raised his head up, and he looked ten years older. Michael knew that Joe's life was back to normal. Joe wouldn't have to bury his kids or grandchildren. He wouldn't spend his life looking for dollar that would give him peace. Michael smiled as he took the glasses off.

Chapter 6

Last Call

The dollar story touched Michael. He began to think of his friend Romy. Michael wanted to know what happened to him. He was reluctant to ask, but he took the chance. "Please tell me what happened to my friend Romy," Michael asked the glasses. The room went dark, and then Michael could see.

Friday night, Romeo walked into the bar. He smiled at the bartender and held up one finger. The bartender smiled back and poured him a pint of beer. Romeo never used his name "Romeo." His mom was a big Shakespeare fan, so he got the name. He went by Romy, and only his mom called his Romeo. As a kid, his mom would call to him, "Oh, Romeo, Romeo, wherefore art thou, Romeo?" His normal response in a half-asleep tone of voice would be "I awake, Mom."

Romy sat down at the corner table. It was his favorite kind of table. It was not a booth or really a table but more like high table with barstools around it. He sat down and looked at the clock and then at the window that showed the back deck. So far, Romy had come to this bar every day this week.

This was his girl's bar. They would come, drink some beers, meet some friends, and go home, forgetting about the day's problems. His girlfriend was his angel. In fact, her name was Angel. He met her when he was a kid. It was at an ice social or carnival that he first saw her. Romy was waiting for his best friend. He didn't see him, so he began to walk around. What would Romy do there? Would he play the dart game, basketball game, or ring toss? He went to the ring toss, and that was when he saw her.

She had a red ribbon in her hair, and she immediately smiled at him. When he saw her, he felt as if he'd been in the cold dark winter his whole life. Now it was as if he stepped into the sunlight. Of course, he didn't say anything because he was totally intimidated by girls. He just smiled and walked away. Lucky for him, she ended up sitting next to him in class the next fall. That was where he found that her name was Angel.

They ended up being friends. He eventually told her how he felt, and she felt the same. They were boyfriend/girlfriend at the start of their teen years, holding hands, passing notes, and talking on the phone. What do kids talk about on the phone? Nothing whatsoever. Mainly, Angel would talk about teen drama, and Romy would listen. He really didn't care about the drama; he just listened to her stories. It was her voice that he wanted to hear, that sweet voice that spoke into his ear like they were the only people in the world. So that was how they went through high school, a fight here and there with a dance sprinkled in between.

Angel went to college about an hour away. Romy stayed at home and got a job. He didn't like school, but he loved working with his hands. While she was away, there were some rough spots, but neither one of them wanted to give up. After Angel graduated from college, they moved into an apartment together. That was their golden age. They both loved their jobs. They would come in this bar with friends and family. Romy's brother, Mike, would hang out with them. Marriage was out there, but neither wanted to push it.

One night three years ago, they were headed to dinner. Romy had a green light as he drove through an intersection. A truck driver who was overworked and drowsy failed to stop at the intersection. Romy's car was knocked clear of the intersection. Six months in a hospital bed was what Romy got. Angel wasn't so lucky. Romy was unconscious for Angel's funeral. After he learned to walk again, he never forgave himself for losing her. So Romy's life became going to work, going home, and avoiding friends. This was how he had lived his life until last Monday.

Last Monday, Romy got off work and headed home. He drove by this bar every day when he would get off work. Something in his heart told him to stop in. He missed that feeling of being around people. Romy wasn't ready for his friends, but strangers were something different.

He walked into the bar and saw the bartender. It was the same guy who used to work there. He ordered a beer and sat over in his corner table. It was his table because Angel decreed that it was one night. She said, "Let it be so. I seal this decree with a judo chop." This memory made him smile.

He looked at the clock and saw it was 6:57 p.m. Romy thought, I could eat. He looked at the menu and debated over the BLT or big bacon burger. Romy made his decision, put down the menu, and looked up. He looked at the large window to the back deck. In his mind, he thought that was where Angel used to smoke, making funny faces and waving to him. To his amazement, he could see her, really see her. She was in the window, smoking.

He thought, That girl looks like Angel. But he remembered those earrings and that hoodie. The hoodie was from the concert at Red Rock.

"It can't be," he whispered to himself. Romy rubbed his eyes, and she was gone. Instantly, he felt sad and happy at the same time. It had been three years, and he can't let her go.

He slammed his beer and got ready to get another when he froze. Opening the door to the back deck was Angel. She walked over to him with a smile, his smile, the smile that she reserved for him. She sat down beside him and gave him a kiss. He could smell her as he hugged her. This felt real, like the last three years never happened—her perfume, the smoke on her hoodie, her soft body against his, and the electricity he always felt when they embraced. "Hey, babe. Jill gave me a ride up here, but she had to split," she said.

Romy hugged her, and she was real. He stuttered, "You're . . . you're . . ."

"Very thirsty. I need a wheat and a bomb. Now remember, I can't pay for these," she said with a smile. He was taken aback by this statement. He instantly remembered a night with her at this bar. They were out with their friends, and she was in rare form. She told the bartender that she needed ten shots. She passed them out to Romy and her friends. Of course, she ordered too much, so she started passing them out to random bar patrons. She gave her toast. "Here's to you, bitches!" And then she slammed the shot.

The bartender said, "That will be sixty dollars."

She then looked at Romy and said, "Romy, I can't pay for these." Romy paid the bill, and the night went on.

The memory faded from him, and he said, "I missed you." She smiled and gave him a kiss.

Romy got up and ordered her drinks. He thought, Is this a dream? Well, if it is, I'll probably wake up if I tell her she died. At that point, he decided to just enjoy the night with her. So they sat, they talked, and they drank. She told her about her day. He told her about his job.

She got up to use the bathroom, and he got nervous. She just smiled and said, "I'm not going anywhere."

The night went on, and he was happy. At about 12:55 a.m., she said, "I'm going to smoke, and then we can go." She walked outside to the deck. He sat at his table, paying the tab. Romy looked up from the table and saw Angel looking through the window. She was smiling his smile at him as she smoked. He looked up at the clock, and it read 12:57 a.m. Just then, he remembered the doctor telling him she died the night of the accident at 12:57 a.m. Romy then saw his Angel wave goodbye and blow a kiss as she faded away. Fighting back the tears, he stood up and walked out.

Romy woke up the next day. He was sad but hopeful. He kept thinking about last night. "If it happened once, it can happen again," he kept telling himself. After work on Tuesday, he drove to the bar, smiled at the bartender, grabbed his beer, and sat at his table. At seven, he looked at the window and saw Angel standing at the window with his smile, smoking a cigarette, and waving. He was relieved, and he hurried to the bar to get her drinks. This time when they talked, it was new conversation topics. This time when she used the "little girls' room," he thought, I'll do this as long as I can.

That would bring us to Friday. Romy sat at his spot and looked out to the window. He noticed that he was early, six thirty early. Romy started watching the baseball game. In the corner of his eye, he saw a man enter the bar. He turned to look and recognized him immediately. It was a man whom he knew his whole life, his brother, Mike. Mike was about four years older than Romy.

Now there are different levels of being a brother. The first level is the baby brother. That's when the elder brother loves or hates the baby brother. The baby brother usually forgets this stage. The second level is the dominant phase. Mike would throw balls, stir food, or just hold him down to beat him up. Now Romy wasn't defenseless. He would flush toilets while Mike was in the shower, have their dog lick his toothbrush, or even hit Mike in the balls with a Wiffle ball bat. Phase 3 is the teen phase. Now the teen phase is usually the safer phase for the younger brother. When a young man becomes a teen, everyone in his life is uncool, especially a little brother. In this phase and all phases, the younger brother sees his elder brother as the pinnacle of coolness; other than his father, this is what he wants to be like. Mike and Romy went through these phases and emerged true brothers with equal respect.

Mike looked around and saw his brother. He walked over to him and gave him a hug. "Hey, man, I missed you," Mike said.

Romy replied, "I missed you too, man. Sorry, I've been working a lot. I meant to call."

Mike gave him a puzzled look and sat down. "So tell me what's going on with you," Mike asked.

"Well, man, I gotta tell you something. Now I'm not crazy. Well, I don't feel crazy. Just hear me out," Romy responded. Mike just nodded. "OK, you know how Angel and I got in that car wreck three years ago. I ended up six months in the hospital learning to walk again. Angel ended up dead, leaving me alone. Well, last Monday, I came here, and I saw her in that window. At seven, she appeared, and we spent the evening here together. I could touch her, and we talked as if nothing happened. At 12:57 a.m., she went outside on the deck and disappeared. It got me thinking about the times. I picked her up at seven that night. The doctor said she died at 12:57 a.m. Since you're here, it probably won't happen. I wish it would because I'm not crazy."

Mike looked at his brother not as if he was crazy but with just an "I miss you" look. Romy waited for his brother to crack a joke or smack some sense into him. Mike just stood up and went to the bar. He came back with three beers. Two of the beers were wheat. Mike said, "We both like wheat." Romy remembered that his brother and Angel both liked wheat.

He thought as he toasted his brother, This guy may think I'm crazy, but we'll be crazy together. Just then, Romy looked at the window, and he could see Angel. "Look there, do you see her?"

"I do, brother," Mike said as he took a long drink.

"No, really, look!" Romy grabbed his brother's arm.

"I see her, man! I'm not messing with you!" Mike exclaimed.

Angel then walked through the door over to Mike. She gave Mike a hug and said she was happy to see him. She told him it felt like old times.

Romy looked at his brother trying to speak. Mike just shook his head and said, "Let's just have a drink and catch up." Romy agreed, and they started talking. Mike told Romy and Angel about his life. The three had laughs, drinks, and talks about old times.

The time of the night Angel used the "little girls' room," Romy noticed something different about his brother. Mike's hairline had receded with a little gray. His face had more lines, and he appeared to be humped over a little. Romy asked his brother, "Dude, are you OK? You look like you've aged twenty years since you sat down."

Mike smiled and said, "Oh, I guess I'm running out of time. Well, brother, there is a reason I'm here. I'm here for you."

Romy replied, "What do you mean?"

Mike put a worn old hand on his brother's shoulder and said, "Angel didn't die. You did. You've been dead a long time. Now to you, it feels like three years, but a lifetime has passed." Romy looked at his brother with disbelief. "Take a drink and let me tell you what happened to Angel. She was in the hospital for months. Eventually, she got better. She was the one who learned to walk again. She never forgot what you two had. Eventually, with help from her friends and family, she moved on with her life.

"Always comparing every man she had a relationship with to you was hard. She ended up with a good man. He made her happy, and they had beautiful kids. We would run into each other from time to time. I got married, had some kids, named one after you, and tried to move on. Nobody ever does though."

Romy looked at his brother, lost. Romy asked, "Then who is that in the bathroom?"

Mike smiled. "That's Angel. You guys loved each other. That's the piece of her soul that she gave you so that you'll never be alone."

"My job, my friends, watching games, and those douchebags I work with that I hate?" Romy questioned.

"Yes, you loved your job. Your friends and family are a part of you. Those guys you hate, well, you really hate them with all your heart." Mike laughed. "Don't worry, those friends you'll see again in another time and place. Like Angel, they gave you a part of themselves." Mike rubbed his back as if hurt from years of work.

"I'll tell you what just happened to me. I died in my bed with my family by my side. When I crossed over, I asked where my little brother was. They brought me here. I'm here to help you move on."

Romy looked to the bathroom, and Angel emerged. She walked over to Romy and asked if it was time to go. Romy said, "I guess, but you can't come."

Mike laughed and said, "Why not? That part of her is a part of you. All you have to do is walk out with me into the unknown."

Romy, scared but trusting his big brother more than anything, stood up. He gave Angel a kiss and whispered something in her ear. Angel smiled and walked out the door to the deck, where she disappeared. Romy helped his brother up, who looked as if he was eighty years old. "Damn, you're old." Romy chuckled.

"Yeah, I got a bum knee and diabetes," Mike snapped back, calling out to the bartender, "Barkeep, how 'bout some traveling music for me and Ugly?" The jukebox instantly turned on, playing Mötley Crüe's "Home Sweet Home."

The two men walked into the night, with the older man relying on the younger one to do most of the work. Outside, halfway through the parking lot, Romy turned to look at the bar. All the lights were off, there was a For Sale sign in the window, and it looked as if it had closed for years. "So do we get to be brothers again? If so, I wanna be the older one."

Mike smiled. "Every life we've had, we are always brothers, and we will always be brothers . . . Ugly." Both men faded away into the night, singing together, "I'm on my way. I'm on my way . . . Home sweet home."

Michael took off his glasses, grabbed a beer from the fridge, and walked outside. He sat on the steps to his front porch. Looking up at the night sky, Michael thought about his brothers. He wasn't happy or sad, just hopeful—hopeful that this endeavor he was on would lead him to a good place. He took a long drink off his beer and stared at the new moon rising in the night sky.

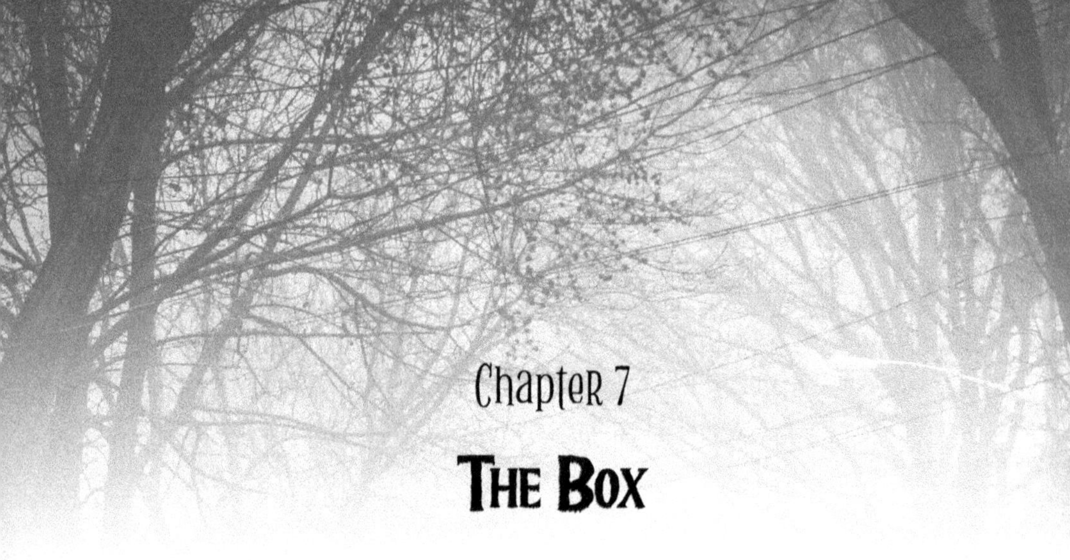

Chapter 7

The Box

Michael never lied to his son. He read him stories when he was younger. Santa Claus, Easter Bunny, and the Tooth Fairy were real because Michael played those parts. When they got a divorce, he told his boy the truth. Jacob didn't like the split, but he learned to live with it. For the first time that Michael could remember, he finally lied. He told his son, Jacob, that he got a new job that would take him all over the world. In a way, he didn't lie. He just didn't tell him the whole truth.

Michael was an independent computer consultant. He would tell his son that he worked at different companies and fixed their IT problems. Jacob would lose interest after hearing that. Lately, Michael would go to the park on his free time. He would use the glasses to escape the pressures of his journey. He would sit on the bench by the big rock. The rock was huge and the most notable landmark of the park. It stood about fifteen feet high and about forty feet in diameter. Burger Rock was what some kids called it because of the shape. Kids would climb on it and play around it.

One day at the park, Michael asked the glasses to show him the park in 1973 on this date. Michael couldn't believe what he saw. Kids were playing on a play set he'd never seen before. It looked like a tepee with a pole in the middle. The pole was longer than the tepee, and it was just the frame. Kids would stand on the outside as the cone would sway back and forth. The merry-go-round was still there, but it had wood inside it. The children would sit on the wood as it turned. This made Michael laugh. He remembered when he held on to the center of a merry-go-round as his buddies pushed it as fast as they could. The clothes the people wore reminded him of The Brady Bunch on TBS. Michael noticed that young hippie teens occupied the rock. Michael could smell the weed coming from them.

He continued to ask the glasses to show him different eras on his free time. Sitting on the bench, watching the park in the '90s, Michael noticed that the glasses suddenly switched back to the current era. He looked over at a tree by the edge of the park. The tree was three times as thick as the ones surrounding it. At the base of the tree, he could see a door form. It was the same door that Patrick used. The door began to open, and a light came from the entrance. He saw Patrick emerge from the door. "Hello, Michael," Patrick said with a smile.

Michael smiled and returned the greeting.

"You've been doing good. I've been watching with great interest. You will be getting your gift soon. First, you must see something. It's important for your journey," Patrick said.

Michael agreed and sat back.

Patrick sat next to Michael and said, "Ask to show you the box."

Michael asked, and the glasses went dark. When the image appeared again, Michael could see the park. All the kids' toys were gone. He figured the time was around the 1920s from the clothes. Michael wasn't sure; he just guessed based on the movies he watched where the clothes were similar. He saw a couple of families in the park having picnics. Michael took a deep breath, and it was clean. It was as if all the pollution in the city was sucked out.

He fixed his attention to a little boy playing with a wooden horse. The little boy had blond hair and blue eyes. His clothes were dirty but not tattered. This little boy liked getting dirty. The boy got up and walked over to the big rock with a tin box. He began to dig a deep hole. It was clear he was going to bury his box. After the boy dug until his arms disappeared, he placed the tin box in. The boy covered the hole up and returned to his family.

Michael asked Patrick who that boy was. Patrick replied, "That boy's name is Jacob, like your boy's name. He is a good person. When he grows up, he'll go to Europe in WWII. He'll save the lives of his friends and liberate civilians. When he comes home, he'll marry his high school sweetheart and have four boys. After thirty years of working in a factory, he retired to the lake. He died in his bed surrounded by his family. That box he buried is for you."

Michael said, "It must be gone." Patrick just pointed to the rock where the box was buried. Michael got up and began to dig.

A while had passed, and Michael had finally hit the tin box. He recovered the box and sat back on the bench. In the front of the box was a cowboy riding a horse in the West. Michael smiled and slowly opened the box. In the box, Michael saw an arrowhead made out of stone or flint and two small leather bags. One bag had a handful of marbles. The other bags had over twenty sharp stones—stones like the arrowhead.

Michael closed the box and looked at Patrick. "Thanks a lot," he said.

"Well, you're welcome. Most of the items you'll collect will fit in the box. I'm going to leave you now. Before I go, I need you to ask if you have a gift. Good luck," Patrick said as he walked back to his door.

Michael watched Patrick disappear into the doorway. He took a deep breath and asked if he had a gift. The glasses went bright and then faded clear. Michael could see a family of three standing in front of a house. Each family member had a box in their arms.

Chapter 8

CAROLINE'S CRAYONS

The three family members stood in front of their new home. It took David and Ann over three years to find the right home. Caroline was excited to get her new room. She wanted her room pink with white stripes. When Caroline had her mind set on something, she wouldn't stop until she got it. After all, she was six and a half. David opened the front door for the ladies. He had a box and their dog, Cooper, on his leash. Cooper (a pug) was a gentleman first and a dog second. He sat on guard until his ladies entered.

The house was a blank canvas. Wood floors covered the house and an out-of-date paint job. Ann didn't mind the paint; she knew what she wanted to do with the house. David was just glad to finally get this over with. They got a good deal on the house. The seller had lost his wife and was moving to Florida. It was almost fate.

Caroline ran to her room and began to talk. David asked, "Are you OK, sugar bear?"

Caroline said, "Yup, Daddy. This room will do."

He smiled at her and walked to the master bedroom. David put his box down and let out a long sigh. He knew that he had a lot of work, but he was happy.

The three of them unloaded their boxes and waited for the moving truck to show up. It did just as Ann was ordering pizza. Caroline and Cooper played in the backyard as the movers quickly moved their stuff. They ate and went to bed after a long day. Cooper slept with Caroline because that was his girl. The good thing about this move was that Caroline didn't have to change schools. That made everyone happy. This was June, so they didn't have to worry about it anyway. David was a teacher at the local high school, and Ann was a nurse at the university hospital.

About a month into living at the house, David was the only one up. He was watching TV in his recliner. Normally, he would watch his shows later at night. Cartoons normally occupied the screen. Sure, Caroline had her own TV, but she and Cooper liked to be around David when Ann was at work. David had the volume low so he wouldn't wake anyone up. He heard a creak in the dining room. "Coop," he whispered. No reply came, and it didn't sound like Cooper. Cooper made little tapping sounds when he walked. This sounded like a slow, shoeless step.

He got up, turned on the lights, and saw nothing. David could feel a cold spot in the room for a second, but then it was gone. He thought, I think that was coming from the front porch. I need to go to bed. David went to bed after he looked in on Caroline and Cooper. He opened the door, and they were both sound asleep.

David closed the door and saw a picture on the door. Caroline had colored a picture of her and Cooper. She was dressed as a knight with a sword and armor. Cooper had his mouth open with lightning coming out of it. David thought they looked fierce. He turned to his room and went to bed.

The next day, the three of them (and Cooper) sat down to breakfast. Caroline was extraexcited today. This was the day she was going to spend the weekend with Charlotte. They were best friends from birth, or so it felt like. Caroline said to her dad with a serious face, "I'm only going to be gone until Sunday, Daddy. If you need me, call."

David smiled and replied, "OK, sugar bear."

"I'm serious, Daddy. Here, take this and let Teddy sleep with you. I don't want him to be lonely," Caroline said as she handed him a picture of Caroline in a karate uniform. She had nunchucks, and her left leg was kicking into the air. Daddy and Mommy were on the couch with Cooper on the other side. Cooper had a machine gun and a red headband.

David laughed and said, "Thank you, baby."

Caroline said, "Put that on your door, and it will protect you."

David smiled and gave her a military salute. He told Caroline to pack her bag. The three of them cleaned the house, waiting for Charlotte and her father to pick her up. Caroline was out the back with Cooper when Ann called out to David.

He walked into Caroline's room and saw Ann holding colored pictures. "What's up?" David asked.

"Look at these. I think she needs less time on her tablet," Ann said.

David held the picture and was taken aback. The images were from a nightmare. One picture was of their house. It was a sunny day with Caroline and Cooper playing in the yard. Under the porch were four dark red circles. Two dark circles were close together like eyes. The other circles were half the size of the closer circles, and they were up on the corners of the closer circles. It looked like a spider's eyes. The second picture was wild. It looked like a web all over the page. He could almost make out a figure of a man and a blob behind him. "Yeah, I'll keep an eye on it," David said as he put the pictures down.

There was a knock on the door, and they both jumped. It was Charlotte and her father. "Hey, guys, we're here," Charlotte's father said. "Dave, I never noticed those stones on your property. I like them.

They look nice. I'm looking for new yard decoration. I think I may do stones like those. Thanks for letting Cooper come over too. These girls love that dog."

David smiled and said, "I can't keep Caroline away from him anyway." Caroline kissed her parents, and they took off.

Ann looked at David and asked him, "Dinner and a movie?" David nodded and smiled at her. They got ready for their date.

Ann went back to Caroline's room and removed her pictures from the folder. Outside, David opened the door for his wife. Ann went to the trunk with pictures in hand. David asked, "What's up?"

"I'm going to show these pictures to Dr. Davis. Maybe he can tell us if anything is wrong." David nodded, and Ann put the pictures into the trunk.

They went to the movies and had dinner with drinks. Returning home, both parents were tired. The house felt empty. Any time Caroline and Cooper were gone, their home felt incomplete. They both had restless sleep.

The next day was an average Saturday. Ann went shopping for crafts. David started his honey-do list. Later that night, they ordered carryout and sat on the front porch. They watched the rain from their porch and had a couple of beers. After a while, they returned into the house as they fell asleep on the couch.

A strike of lightning woke them up. The lights in the front room were off. The only light was from the kitchen. David heard a tapping on the front porch. It didn't sound like feet or shoes. The sound was as if someone was walking on wooden stilts. Confused, they got up and walked outside on the front porch. It was beautiful. It wrapped around to the side of the house, covered. From the floor to the ceiling was about eight feet. They stood outside, looking across the porch. The neighborhood was dark as if the storm knocked out the lights. Ann and

David looked at the end of the porch where it began to wrap around. "Hello?" David questioned. They squinted because they were confused about what they saw.

It looked as if a man was kneeling on a table. They had no tables on the porch. The thing he was on was tall, so tall that his head almost touched the top of the porch ceiling. A strike of lightning lit up the porch, and they were aghast. It wasn't a man on a table but a man combined with a giant spider, a centaurlike creature; but instead of a horse, it was a giant spider. As it walked forward, they could see the light from the kitchen was still working. The light bled through the window into the creature. Its leg stretched across the porch, holding up its hairy dark body. It turned slightly, and they could see the bloated abdomen connected to the forebody. The hair that covered it was coarse and black. The hair climbed up the creature's torso to the human-looking part. Corpselike white skin covered the human segment. Its arms were long with nail-like fingers projecting from its hands. The face was on a humanoid head. Four dark red eyes stared at them. No mouth could be seen until another lightning strike. Its mouth opened from its jawline like a vise being slowly cranked open six inches, one foot, and then two feet. The teeth were sharp like dark brown icicles.

Ann screamed as David pushed her inside. He locked the door and held it closed. Ann grabbed her phone and dialed 911. They heard the creature scurrying across the porch to the door. Ann said, "Please answer."

David said, "Tell them home invasion. They won't believe this. I don't believe this!"

Ann screamed, "Help! He's trying to get in! We're holding the door closed!"

The dispatch repeated their address as Ann kept saying, "Yes, come . . . yes, come."

David screamed, "Grab the fireplace poker! If it gets in, run out the back!"

Ann began to cry as she held the poker. The door handle jiggled. Then it went quiet. They both stopped everything, even breathing. A voice from outside the door whispered, "The itsy-bitsy spider climbed up the waterspout. Down came the rain and washed the spider out. Out came the sun." There was laughter. "Now, David, you'll never see the sun."

A siren came closer and closer. Suddenly, they heard the creature scurrying across the porch. Police lights shone through the windows. The officer knocked on the doors. At first, they didn't want to open, but David finally did. The police checked the house, under the porch, and in the neighborhood. After a couple of hours of reports, the rains had stopped. The couple stayed awake until the sun came up. Ann told David that they were moving.

Around noon, Caroline had come back home. "I'm back!" she called.

Ann and David ran to meet her at the door. "What's going on?" Caroline asked.

Ann said, "We're not spending one more night here."

"Why, Mama?" Caroline asked.

"There was a bad man who came here and—" Ann said until Caroline cut her off.

"Mama, did you move my pictures?"

They both looked at her, confused.

"I know about that creepy spider. He came to my window the second night we moved in here. I told him to leave me alone. He laughed at me. So I colored him into a picture. I put him into my folder. He begged me to release him from the floor. I told him if I heard him again, I would burn his picture. Don't worry, Daddy, I wasn't going to play with fire. I told him that to scare him like when you say you're going to spank me. After that, not a peep. If he got out from under the porch, you must have moved my picture."

Her parents were stunned to silence. "Daddy, if you make hot dogs tonight, you can burn my picture. That will make him go away," Caroline said with complete confidence.

Cooper gave a bark. "Cooper would like a hot dog too," she said with a smile.

Ann slowly got up and retrieved the pictures. David started the grill as Caroline and Cooper played with bubbles. The hot dogs were made, and Ann placed the pictures into the fire. Ashes flew up ten feet high. Ann and David looked at the porch and saw ashes rising from under the porch to join the paper ashes. The ashes floated to the street. When they reached the street, they floated against the wind toward the woods. "Mama, I promise he won't be back. Let's sleep on moving," Caroline said.

"OK, baby, one night." Ann looked at David.

That night, Caroline slept in between David and Ann with Cooper on the floor. Caroline wanted to sleep in her room, but Ann insisted. That night, Ann and David had wonderful dreams. They had no fear and woke up feeling safe. It was like they were kids and it was Christmas morning. Ann didn't want to move and didn't know why. Any normal person who saw a giant half man, half spider would.

Ann went to the fridge and looked on the door. Caroline had colored a picture of them. The picture had the family together hugging and happy. There were no eyes under the porch. The sun was shining, and flowers bloomed. Ann pulled the picture down and put it in a frame. She placed it to the fireplace mantel. David hugged Ann as Caroline ate her cereal in the kitchen.

Michael took off the glasses, white as a ghost. "Drider, why did it have to be a drider?" He remembered when he was a boy and played D&D. In Dungeon and Dragons, a drider is a half man, half spider. He could never defeat a drider.

Michael stared into nothing, and then he noticed that the glasses were trying to show him something. He put them back on and saw the grocery store he found the glasses at. "OK," he said to himself. He stood up and walked to his car. Michael pulled up to the store and walked toward the entrance. As he approached, he was taken aback. There they were, sitting at a table by the entrance.

Caroline and Charlotte had Girl Scout vests on behind a stack of cookies. David was off to the side, talking to a parent. "Greetings, my good man," Caroline said. "Would you like some cookies?"

Michael said, "Absolutely." Boxes were exchanged, and both parties couldn't stop smiling.

"Here, Mister," Caroline said as she held a small box. Michael took the box and realized what they were. They were crayons in a small box, the kind of crayons they give kids at a restaurant to keep them busy— red, blue, and green with a cowboy on both sides of the box. He could tell that Caroline drew the cowboys.

"If you ever get scared, draw what scares you, and you'll be OK," Caroline said.

Michael thanked her and walked back to his car. He opened the door and looked at the intersection. For a second, he thought he saw a man drive by, staring at him. The man was wearing a mask—no, not a mask, a face, a mannequin's face.

Chapter 9

Private Eye

Slowly opening his eyes, Detective Wilson realized that he was tied up in a chair. He can't see anything because it was pitch black. Where was he, and how did he get there? The lights came on, and it hurt his eyes. He was in a basement that had earth walls. A tall figure passed him and sat at a wooden table with an old typewriter. Looking at this person, he knew this was the man he was supposed to find. "Hello, Detective Wilson," the man said.

Detective Wilson can't believe what he was seeing. Jenni gave a description of this man to a T. He was dressed in an old suit with spandex underneath, covering his whole body. His mask was what crept him out the most, that cutoff mannequin's face with sunglasses and no emotion.

"As you can tell, you are not gagged. So please don't yell. No one will hear you. I just want to talk to you for now," he said.

Detective Wilson nodded.

"Good. My name is E. Charles Grant. You may call me E." E. started to read some papers left on the table. "I see that you have been looking for me, ex-police-detective turned private eye. You are very good, very close to finding me. I see you have talked to my ex-landlord. Too bad for him." He put down the papers.

"If I can find you, someone else will too," Detective Wilson said.

"Oh, I believe you. It will be harder with my ex-landlord out of the picture," E. said as he stood up and began to walk around him. "Do you like children? I do. I don't mean like a creep. Kids will have no fear of jumping a dirt bike ramp but scared of the closet monster. I am scared of children, one child in particular in our fair city. This girl has certain gifts. I try to stay away from her. She has the power to kill a monster like me. I've seen what she can do. She destroyed a beautiful creature of night with crayons."

Detective Wilson thought, This guy is crazy. The room smelled of blood and mildew. The detective knew that this crazy guy was messing with him and that he was in trouble.

"Detective, this part of my tale to you is important. It will directly affect you. Now this little girl loves her mommy and daddy. They went to the movies last week. I have no desire to do battle with her yet. She is way too powerful for me. What I did do is save the descendant of a mighty race. The night they left for the movies, I went to their home. I didn't enter the home. I merely crawled under the porch. Under the porch, I was able to recover a softball-sized sack. This sack was dried out. Think of it as a dehydrated creature. All you need to grow this beautiful beast is blood. Don't worry, you won't hatch this little ducky. I have a special person for that," E. said.

He walked back to the desk and sat down. He opened a drawer in the desk. E. pulled out the sack that looked like a spider's egg sack. The egg sack was being held in a human skull. The skull had been broken in half to look like a bowl. The person whose skull this was had brown hair. Detective Wilson knew he was going to die. "OK, you're crazy, and you're probably going to kill me. What do you want?" Detective Wilson said.

"Detective Wilson, I promise I will not end your life. You're right, I'm crazy—crazy to see what he's going to do," E. said. He put the sack down and walked behind the detective. "Sacrifices in our lives define us. I believe that your sacrifice will be remembered."

Detective Wilson felt a sharp pain in his neck, and the lights went dark. He started to wake again. He was tied to a tree in the woods. His arms were wrapped backward around the tree in a hug as his back was pressed against it. In his mouth was a rag tied around his mouth, not allowing him to speak. His feet were dangling against the tree. He was about two feet high. Looking across from him, he saw a man in the exact same position that he was in. Detective Wilson knew this man. He was Mr. E.'s ex-landlord. He looked around and saw he was deep in the woods. There were no trails, and all he heard were birds.

E. walked into view. "Hello. We are now at our second site. I do believe you know Mr. James. Mr. James does not believe in confidentiality. Mr. James is a good landlord though. So I thought I'd give him one last tenant." E. walked over to Mr. James and opened his button shirt. Above his belly button was a long scar with fresh stitches. Under his skin was the shape of a ball by the stitches. Mr. James looked out of it. Detective Wilson was glad that Mr. James was out of it. Awake, the pain would be excruciating.

E. pulled out a ziplock bag that contained blood. He started to pour it around Detective Wilson's feet. Detective Wilson thought, If this guy leaves me out here, I may be able to slip out. In amazement, Detective Wilson saw the ball move, a little at first and then more and more like larvae.

"There he goes. He's beginning to eat. He'll eat and eat until it's time to come out. When he escapes his meat cocoon, he'll still be hungry. That's where you come in, Detective. You're his next meal. Then he'll eat whatever he wants," E. said with joy in his voice. "Goodbye, Detective Wilson." He injected the detective with a syringe.

As the detective slowly slipped back into sleep, he saw E. took off his glasses. He saw the mannequin's face with eyes not cut out. Detective Wilson thought as he fell asleep, How does he see?

Hours later, Detective Wilson woke up. Sharp pains came from his wrist and shoulder. It looked like the sun was setting, but he could not see it. Across from him, Mr. James was halfway there. His ribs down was on the ground or gone. Claw marks were on his chest and face. Detective Wilson looked around and saw nothing.

He started moving his arms back and forth. Mr. Wilson felt the ropes rubbing against the tree. He started to remember when he was a boy in Boy Scouts. Making a fire with a stick and rope was one of his favorite things to do. The troop leader would tell him that this could save his life one day. He truly believed that the Boy Scouts may be right. Back and forth, he felt the ropes loosen. "Almost there," he said to himself.

He then felt something poking the top of this head. He closed his eyes out of fear. This felt like a thick twig, one and then two twigs. Two twigs turned into four. He opened his eyes and saw a furry body and spiderlike abdomen. The spiderlike creature was the size of a small dog. It pushed off his face and dangled in front of him. The dog-sized spider had a doll-shaped figure opposite the abdomen. It didn't look real until the face turned to look at him. Its four red spider eyes glowed furiously at him. The creature hung by its long web out of its abdomen. Mr. Wilson just stared at it in terror. He felt like it was waiting for the sun to go down, savoring his fear at the moment. It just hung in front of his face, swinging in the wind as the light began to fade.

Chapter 10

The Burglars

"This is it. This score will pay us plenty. I've been watching this house for over a year. They are normally home, not now. They are gone," Jesse said to his fellow burglars. He was the leader. He did time for assault, breaking and entering, and narcotics. Jesse lived in this city his whole life. He hated it, but he would never leave it. Cody had known Jesse since high school. They dropped out together. Cody would follow Jesse anywhere. In fact, Cody went to jail with Jesse a few times. Jesse and Cody were the actual burglars, and Levi was the lookout. Levi was nineteen years old, and he wasn't the smartest guy you ever met. He followed Jesse's orders, so that was enough.

Levi sat in the alley behind the house in the car. It was the car of Jesse's girlfriend, and he used it whenever he wanted. Jesse's girlfriend thought she loved him, but she was actually just afraid of being alone. When Jesse was in jail, she liked the attention she got from her friends. One day he'd go away for a long time, and she'd realize how lucky she was to be rid of him.

Jesse and Cody entered the backyard at about nine. Most of the people in the neighborhood were at work or very old. The neighbors to these soon-to-be victims were both at work. Victims were on vacation. Mrs. Victim went to a gym where they had a contest to see who would lose the most weight in sixty days. She won the contest, beating Mrs. I'm Better Than You Since High School. Beating this lady made Mrs.

Victim very happy because her family now got to go on a well-deserved vacation, and the lady she beat was fatter than she was.

Cody used a pry bar to enter the back door to gain entry. They both entered, knowing that this family did not have a burglary alarm. They separated in the house. Jesse went upstairs while Cody worked the downstairs. Jesse went straight to the master bedroom. Jewelry and electronic devices were swiftly taken. Jesse looked for a gun in the closet and in different spaces. Cody did pretty much the same thing. He stayed low in case he was seen by a passing car in the front window of the house. There was no money, no jewelry but DVD players. He stayed away from the TV. A sixty-five-inch TV would be hard to carry out. Jesse also told him before every burglary, "No TVs. TVs are bad luck for me."

The dozen or so burglaries that Jesse committed, he got caught every time he took a TV. With a thirty-two-inch TV, he was caught in the alley by an overweight cop named Johnson. With a fifty-five-inch TV, he was caught at Walmart two hours later by the cops and a nosy neighbor. Ever the superstitious person, Jesse said, "No TVs."

Both men met up in the living room after the haul they got from the residence. Jesse looked through the windows and saw a police car turn into the alley. "Shit," Jesse said with a whisper.

Cody asked, "What do we do?"

Jesse looked at Cody and said, "Levi is on his own. Let's jump the fence to the woods, and we'll hide until they are gone. We can walk east until we hit the park." Both men crouched out of the back door, jumped the fence, and disappeared into the woods.

Levi sat in the car as the police officer approached. "Is there a problem, son?" the officer asked.

Levi said, "Nope."

"What are you doing here?" the officer asked.

"Do you know that Missy on the next block over? Well, her old man is about to leave so this young man can handle some business," Levi said.

The police officer started to laugh because all the officers in the area knew Missy. "OK, stud, none of my business. Just don't get caught. I don't want to do a homicide investigation where you are the victim and her old man is the suspect."

Levi smiled. "I'll boogie on outa here for a minute, sir." The police officer tipped his hat and backed out of the alley.

Jesse and Cody walked deeper into the woods. "I think the park is this way," Jesse said. Cody nodded and followed his fearless leader. They walked for an hour, and Cody felt like they were walking in circles.

"I think we passed this area before. That rock looks familiar," Cody said.

"Oh, Cody, so you've seen it before. Where, at a bar?" Jesse said with utter contempt for Cody.

"Man, I think we're lost," Cody replied, trying to hide his fear.

The two men kept walking deeper and deeper into the woods. The woods were very large. They linked up to the county park. If you were unlucky, you could walk two days in one direction and still be in the woods. You would simply walk into a wildlife preserve. They took a break at a stream. Both men drank from the stream. Jesse looked at Cody and said, "Phone?"

"You said no phones on jobs. They can trace you. Plus, a phone is a little TV."

Jesse looked at Cody and then motioned him to move on. They walked in the wood, and day grew dim. When they first started out, it was an overcast day. It looked like rain, but it only misted. The trees and the cloud cover made the day darker than it was. "What is that?" Cody asked.

"That's spiderwebs," Jesse responded.

"It looks like white cotton candy," Cody said. The spiderwebs were thick and blocked the way of a path. The men chose the other path. They continued to walk what seemed like a path, steering clear of the giant spiderwebs.

"It must take spiders a long time to make that much web," Cody said.

"Yup, or it's a big-ass spider."

An hour or so later, Cody said, "We're going in a circle, Jesse."

"Oh yeah? How can you tell?" Jesse responded back with a "stop being scared" tone.

"Look, I put my initials into this stone when we took a break. Here they are," Cody said with alarm.

"OK, we're lost. What do we do now?" Jesse said without even looking at him. "Well, ain't you even going to say anything?" Jesse turned around and looked at Cody. Cody was just standing there with a blank look on his face. "Hey what's wrong with you?" He approached him. Jesse then stopped when he saw two long black fingers come from behind Cody's back. Cody then fell to his knees. Jesse could see what was behind him.

A five-foot creature emerged. The creature was a large hairy black spider at the bottom and a corpse of a man at the top. The head had four dark red eyes that glowed. The man part of the monster was holding

Cody by his spine. "What the!" Jesse screamed as the creature ripped out Cody's spine. Jesse ran blindly into the woods, screaming.

Not looking where he was going, he ran into one of the spiderwebs. The web was stronger than Jesse thought it should be. He tried to break free, but it felt like he was wrapped in duct tape all over his body. Stuck on the web, he could hear the creature coming closer and closer. The creature sounded like a giant cicada. Jesse was able to see only with his right eye. The other eye was buried into the web. He saw the creature dragging Cody's body. It laid his body next to Jesse. With a muffled scream, Jesse watched as the creature covered the rest of his body with a web cocoon.

Chapter 11

Facing the Drider

Michael returned home after his encounter with Caroline. He placed the crayons in the tin box and got a glass of water from the tap. Drinking his water, he had a bad feeling in his heart. He turned around and saw that his glasses were active. They were sitting on the counter, and the inside of the lenses were bright. They looked like headlights on a dark road.

He carefully put them on. He could see himself as if he was the star of a movie he was watching in the third person. Standing in front of his kitchen table, he had the tin box open. He grabbed six stones and two marbles. Michael saw himself put the glasses into the box. In the back jeans pocket was Jacob's slingshot. He also saw a bandanna stuffed into his pocket. Michael knew that this was a test that he had to do alone. The image faded, and one of the park appeared past the swings to the edge of the forest. He saw himself pass through some bushes to discover a path.

The image faded again back to his kitchen. He knew where to go and to go now. Michael did as the glasses asked. Déjà vu, he thought as he grabbed his rocks and marbles.

Looking around, he remembered the bandanna. "Do I have one? Yes, in the boy's room," Michael said to himself. He went to the boy's right sock drawer. That was where he stored his junk. He opened the drawer and found it balled up in the back corner. Michael shook it out, and something fell that was wrapped in it. Looking down, he saw it was his Dungeon and Dragons die from when he was a boy. The die rested on a four.

Laughing to himself, he thought, I would need more than a four. He rolled the die again. On the third roll, he stopped and picked up the die. He realized that he should probably hold on to the die after rolling three times in a row with a twenty-side die.

"OK, four, I'll remember that number," Michael said to the die. He shoved the bandanna into his pocket and headed out with his boy's slingshot as his weapon.

Driving to the park, he thought of nothing but the song on the radio. The pit of his stomach was heavy, but he knew that this had to be done. When he got to the park, there were about half a dozen people. He walked across the park to the bushes where he should enter. Pushing his way through the bushes, he emerged on the other side to see the path. Slowly, he made his way down.

As he walked, he remembered a story on the news about this area. They did a human-interest story about homeless camps. People were living down here in tents. A community group was complaining about it because they were afraid they would do something to the kids at the park. Nothing ever happened to any kids at the park. Thinking of this, he suddenly could smell human waste.

He continued to a clearing where he saw three or four tents scattered around. One of the tents looked as if the top had been torn open. For a minute, he thought the people living here were just messy, but then he saw the campfire tossed about. He saw pile of dirty clothes next to it. A few moments later, he realized that it was a man. The man was missing body parts. Michael walked closer past the largest tent to see his horror.

Bent over was the drider. It was feasting on a man. The man was dead and was being devoured by this creature. Michael could see the bloated, hairy abdomen of the beast. His corpselike human skin was stained with blood. As it ravenously tore into the dead man, Michael slowly pulled out his slingshot. Grabbing a stone, he took aim. "The head," he whispered to himself, pulling back, aiming, and then releasing. The stone flew straight into the creature's shoulder, embedding itself like a stone into mud.

Dropping the body, the drider lifted its whole body to deliver a bloodcurdling cicada-like scream. The drider raised on four of its eight furry legs. It slammed down, shaking the ground and dropping Michael to his back. Michael hurried to grab another stone from his pocket as the seven-foot half man, half spider ran toward him.

The giant creature knocked a tree down over Michael. The tree wasn't heavy, but its branches were thick enough to keep the creature's arms from grabbing him. Michael pulled back the slingshot as he was under the tree and creature. He looked at the creature's dark red eyes and thought, Four, the creature's eyes, four of them. Michael rolled a four. Shoot the eyes! Letting go of the slingshot, knowing that he had one last shot, Michael was frozen. The stone flew into the inner right eye. A gray pus squirted out as the creature fell to the side.

Michael climbed out from under the tree and stared at the monster. Michael pulled out another stone as the creature began to roll. He realized that it was dead, but the camp was on a grade. The creature's speed began to increase toward a clearing where it disappeared over a cliff. Michael ran over to see a forty-foot drop. At the bottom was a shallow creek. There were lots of trash and cans probably from the homeless camp. The creature's body had burst open, with blood and guts being washed away with the creek water.

A sharp pain came from his right shoulder. It was cut by the tree or the creature. He reached into his pocket for the bandanna. Michael could feel something warm in his hand. He pulled out a marble. Lying in the palm of his hand, the inside of the multicolored marble began to swirl. It looked like a mini-gas-giant, Jupiter or Saturn in the palm of his hand. It swirled faster and faster until it faded clear like a bubble. Pop! The bubble exploded in his hand.

Michael then noticed that his shoulder wasn't hurting anymore. He examined his wound, and nothing was there but some torn clothes. Michael smiled with a sigh. He turned and walked away. He saw that the creature's body wouldn't be there long. Plus, he wasn't going down there.

Michael walked back to his car and went home. Down in the creek, the creature's head lay on a rock busted open. A figure emerged from the trees. The figure plunged his gloved hand into the creature's right eye to remove Michael's stone. Washing it in the creek, the figure held the stone to its plastic mannequin's face.

Chapter 12

TREE DEMON

Helen was lying on her bed, trying to finish her romance novel. It was one of those stories where the hero says all the right things and probably doesn't forget to take out the trash. She can't concentrate, but tree branches were scratching outside her window. The wind was pretty strong tonight, and she remembered that her car was parked outside the garage. It was in the back of her house. She normally parked in front of it on the long driveway that wrapped around the side of her house.

A large crash came from where her car was parked. "Jack, can you check on my car? I think a tree may have fell on it!" Helen called to her husband.

Jack slowly got up and walked to the back door. "Yeah, yeah!" he called to her.

Jack walked out into the windy night. A branch was covering the entire hood of her car and hung over the passenger's side, where Jack could not see. He grabbed the thin branches and tried to pick them up but was unable to. Confused, he tried again. He thought, What's going on? This can't be right. They must weigh ten pounds, but they feel like a hundred.

Jack walked over to the passenger's side to see if the branches were hung up on something. He then realized that the branches were stuck to him. They seemed to be holding on to him. Jack then felt his arms going up. He was being pulled up by the branches. "Shit." He was getting pulled up by the wind. He then called out to Helen. "Helen, I'm stuck! I'm getting pulled—"

At that time, Jack looked into the eyes of something. It was a tree but with eyes. The head looked like a praying mantis. It was holding Jack up to its face. Before Jack could call out again, its mouth with hundreds of wooden stakes for teeth bit Jack in half. The creature backed up into the trees and vanished into the woods. A few seconds later, Helen opened the back door and called out to Jack. He did not respond.

Michael was sitting at his favorite coffee shop, video-chatting to his son, Jacob. Jacob was on vacation with his mother. He missed his son, but he would rather him be away from this area. After a long conversation, Michael hung up and finished his coffee. He drove to the park and headed to his bench.

He was surprised to see Patrick sitting on the bench, feeding some birds. "Hello, Michael. I'm very proud of you. I almost thought that creature had you."

"Thanks. I'm glad I didn't get eaten by a giant spider. So what's next?" Michael said not so enthusiastically.

"Well, you have a problem. The next test you have was locked up in the county park. Your city council decided to move some pretty important stones, so it's free," Patrick said.

"The tree?" Michael said quietly.

"Yes, the Tree Demon. His kind hates people. That is why they are locked up. Since this one got out, he has killed many people. You will need extra help. I need to go the county park and meet with the caretaker. He is retiring soon, but he will give you help. His name is Mr. Blackfoot. Ask Mr. Blackfoot for Bear Claw's savior. He'll ask where you heard that. Tell him a friend named Patrick," Patrick explained. Michael got up, walked to his car, and headed toward the county park.

Michael pulled up to the caretaker's cabin. Chills raced down his spine. He remembered the kids with the Tree Demon. He knocked on the door, and Mr. Blackfoot answered. "Hello, can I help you?" he said.

"Yes, sir, my name is Michael."

"Hello, Michael, how can I help you?" Mr. Blackfoot said.

"This may sound strange, but I'm looking for Bear Claw's savior. Patrick sent me," Michael said.

Mr. Blackfoot smiled and motioned Michael to enter. "How tall was Patrick?" he questioned.

Michael, using his hand, showed him.

Mr. Blackfoot smiled and closed the door after Michael entered. He asked Michael to take a seat and grabbed two bottles of soda. They both sat across from each other. Mr. Blackfoot started, "Bear Claw was a brave man some time ago. He met your friend Patrick. He was given a great gift and a great quest. Bear Claw had to destroy a great evil, the ones that have no names. Bear Claw used this. This was able to kill one of his kind."

Mr. Blackfoot held up a stone tomahawk. "This great weapon was passed from generation to generation in case someone needed to cast out those demons." He handed the tomahawk to Michael. "I gave this tomahawk to a man recently. He said the same thing you have said. He was given the history on this weapon. The man entered the county park and never returned. I recovered the weapon buried in a tree."

Michael looked the tomahawk and squeezed it tight.

"Good luck, my friend. I hope you'll return it when you're done."

Michael smiled and left the cabin. He drove back to his home, only thinking of the task he must complete.

Pacing back and forth in his living room, E. was visibly upset. His face was covered by his mannequin's mask, but he was not happy. "I know, I know. He's not going to live through the tree," he said to a figure sitting in the corner. It was the mannequin whose face was missing. He was dressed up in a dirty old suit. E. responded to him as if he was talking to him.

"I know, I did what was asked of me. That homeless vet, I put him out of his misery. Milcom said I needed the masher. He'll have the masher in the end. That's the key," he said, still pacing around. "The masher will solve all my problems." E. walked down toward his basement. He closed the door behind him, and you can barely hear someone call out "help."

Jason checked his pulse as he ran down the street. He'd been training for a 5K coming up in the fall. He ran the same path for his training. Part of his path ran by the woods. He liked this part of his run, not a lot of cars and lots of nature. The road was flat but had a steep embankment on the deep woods' side. Listening to his ear pods, he suddenly lost connection. He came to a stop and looked at his phone. It had shut off. "Damn," he said to himself. Jason tried to reset his phone when he heard it.

"Help!" A young voice came from the woods. Jason looked at the tree line. He knew that voice.

"Chance?" Jason called out.

"Yes, it's me, Mr. Lawson! It's Chance! Help!" the boy said.

"Where are you?" Jason said.

"I'm here behind some trees. I was riding my dirt bike and wiped out. I think I broke my leg," the boy's voice uttered with fear.

Jason knew this boy. He cut his yard and lived a couple of houses down. Chance was a bit of a daredevil. He was always taking his bike off jumps. Jason knew there was a bike path in the woods. He slid down the embankment and pushed his way through the thick brush. Finally, he reached a clearing. He saw a bike lying on the path. It looked as if it was blocked by some thorn bushes. "I'm here behind this tree," the boy said.

As he came around the tree, he saw eyes. They glowed white at Jason as it stared at him. Jason heard the boy's voice coming from the creature as it stood nearly two stories high. "Sorry, Mr. Lawson, he ate me earlier today, but he's still hungry."

Jason backed up to realize that the torn bushes had blocked him in. He looked up to see the creature's mouth open to reveal its hundreds of stakelike teeth. Instantly, the creature bit Jason. He had been swallowed halfway, leaving his kneecaps hanging from its mouth. The creature finished its meal as it laughed using the boy's voice.

Michael returned home and noticed that he had a message on his phone. He called the number back and spoke with Joe. Joe was the IT guy at the last job he did. "Hey, Michael, I was wondering if you would be willing to help us with some work. A network that we are associated with has a reality show in town. They are set up, but they are having technical issues. Double the standard rate, but it's only for the weekend. Are you interested?" Joe asked.

Michael put on his glasses and said, "This weekend? Looks like I'm helping you out. Go ahead and give them my information."

Michael put down the phone and grabbed his backpack. He placed the tomahawk into the bag along with other items. He knew this was it. This would be his encounter with the Tree Demon.

The next day, Michael ended up on the west side of Lyons Park. The street he went down to meet his clients was almost abandoned. Only two houses were occupied on this dead end. The two occupied houses were on the corner. Both had senior citizens in their nineties. The rest of the six houses were unfit and abandoned. Vacant lots dotted the block. The dead end of the street had a trail that led to the park. Local schoolkids would park on the dead end and hang out.

The last house on the dead end was where Michael's clients would be working. The house was one of the oldest houses in town. It was owned by Edward Lyon. He donated the land for the park when he died. The house was kept up by the rec department. The ghost story of the house was that Mr. Lyon haunted the house. He was mad because his child disappeared in what was now the county park. In front of his house was a statue of this daughter. She was holding a bird in her hands. The way the statue was made, when it rained, her hands filled with water. Local birds used it as a birdbath. The stone the statue was made of was found locally, like the ones around the county park.

Michael pulled up to the house and saw a van. It had "Scare Crew" on the side. Michael started to laugh, remembering the show this name was associated with. The show followed a ghost-debunking crew. They used state-of-the-art technology to detect spiritual energy. Apparently, Michael was called out to fix their ghost computers. He walked up to the van just as it opened. "Hi there. Are you Michael?" an older man said.

"Yes, I'm here to help you with your tech," Michael replied.

"Good, we've been having problems with it. I'm Craig, and I'll introduce you to the crew."

Both men walked past the statue. Michael noticed a red-bellied woodpecker resting on its head. Jacob had done a paper on that bird for school, and that was how he knew it. The bird tilted its head at them as it looked at both men as if the bird were trying to tell the men to leave.

Michael met the rest of the crew and got to work. He was able to restore their computers, but he stuck around on the request of the crew. The cast was three people—Craig, April, and Johnny. The crew had two tech guys (Allan and Steve) and security. The security was a retired police officer named Nick.

As it got dark, Craig told Michael about their last job. They stayed in a house where a man had killed people who sucked at karaoke. Apparently, he would go to the local bar. The people who really couldn't hold a tune were his victims. He would kidnap them and bury them in the basement. Part of the equipment was a karaoke machine. Craig would ask the spirits if they were still there and if they wanted to sing a song. April said "Sweet Caroline" got the most kinetic energy. Michael then said, "Ba, ba, ba, good times never felt so good." They laughed, and the night went on.

Craig and Michael began to long conversation. "How did you start doing this job?" Michael asked Craig.

"Well, I kind of fell into this job. Every one of us has a personal ghost story except Johnny. He's doing this for the money. My story involves childhood friends. It messed me up, but with therapy, I can talk about it. I like talking about it. The more you tell a story, the more it becomes just a story. You want to hear it?" Craig asked. Michael nodded and took a drink from his cola.

Craig's Tale

"When I was a boy, I loved to play sports. I guess I loved to play anything. Football, basketball, and baseball would be my activities year-round. When I wasn't playing those games, I would hang out with my friends. We would compete with one another and see who could swim the fastest or who could run the fastest. We would also test our nerves. We would see who was the bravest. We did Bloody Mary in the mirror to see who could last in the basement with no lights the longest by themselves. I look back and realize that the games we played were stupid. Jumping off a cliff to the water could have gotten us seriously hurt.

"The most bizarre and frightening thing I ever done still haunts me today. It was the summer before we started high school. We rode our bikes all over the city. Every day we would pass the old Farris house. This house was the haunted house of our community. No one had lived in the house for years. The legend goes that Mr. Farris was into devil worship. His wife had left him and took his three daughters. This drove him crazy.

"One day he was gone. No one saw him move. The neighbors went over with the police, and the house was empty. All his stuff was still there. The house stood empty for years. At first, kids who liked stealing would sneak into the house and take what they wanted. This is where the story gets changed around, but the legend says that when kids would take something, the next night, they would get a visitor. If the kid didn't return the stolen item, they would disappear. Pretty creepy, right?

"One day that summer, we went to the house. We parked our bike in the alley and snuck in between the missing pieces of fence. On the back of the house was spray paint. Kids painted stuff like 'Where's Tommy?' 'Let Ginger go!' and pentagrams. We went in through the back door. The house was a typical haunted house—old furniture, cobwebs, and stained wallpaper. It smelled of mildew, rotting animals, and urine. My buddies didn't want to split up. So we went upstairs to grab a token. The creepy part of this is that when I look back, I still can't believe that money was still in the house. He had a change mug on his dresser. People and kids were so convinced that if they stole anything, they would not like it. My best friend, Chris, told me that he's wasn't taking anything because he wasn't a thief. I think part of this was his morals, but I also think he was scared. John didn't care. He took the change in the mug. I put a thimble in my pocket. We all wrote our initials in the doorjamb in one of the kids' rooms. We left the house and felt like we did something.

"That night, Chris spent the night at my house. John went to see some family and would be out of town for a couple of days. I put the thimble by my rock collection. We forgot about it as the night went on. That night, we did what we always did when one would spend the night. We ate pizza, played video games, and talked about girls. My dad worked nights, and my mom has trouble sleeping, so she would take sleeping pills. We stayed up as long as we could.

"At around 3:00 a.m., the power went out. We both were pissed at first because we thought we lost our spot in the game. My room was on the first floor, and my mom and dad's was upstairs. I mentioned that maybe we should go to bed. Chris asked if I heard a noise. I told him to cut it out when his face went white. I turned and looked out the window. At fourteen, most kids have the curtains open late at night in case you need to sneak out. I saw a man in the window, not the outline of a man, a real fucking man. He was completely hairless, no eyebrows and nothing on his head. His mouth looked like someone tried to sew it closed. His eyes were wide open, and he looked only at me. With his long fingers, he pointed to my shelf. Finally, we both screamed and ran out to the hall.

"That was it. We looked back after what seemed like forever, and he was gone. We fell asleep in the living room. My parents think it was a nightmare. That next day, we both went back, and I put that thimble where I got it. I remember a note written on the dresser where I left the thimble. I don't remember seeing the note the first time, but memories are funny like that. The note said, 'Don't ever come back.' We didn't hear anything I can remember. I just know we flew out of that place.

"When John came home, we told him what happened. He blew us off. I guess he thought we were trying to scare him. He told us that he couldn't bring back the change anyways. John had spent it a carnival. The next day, my friend John went missing. The police were called, and they tried to blame it on one of the carnival workers. A couple of years in therapy for Chris and me. I ended up being a haunted house debunker. Thank god they tore down that house years ago for a new housing development because I wasn't going back. This job be damned."

Michael slapped Craig's back and smiled.

"Let's get back to work," Craig said. Michael watched the crew do their jobs, knowing that they would probably be bait for the Tree Demon.

The night went on as the crew recorded themselves talking out loud to the ghost of the house. "Give us a sign. Talk to us and tell us why you're mad. Did you find your daughter? Let us help you, Edward. Do want people to stay out of your house? You donated the park. Are you happy with the park?" Craig said.

Michael sat in the computer room with the generators humming, watching the monitors. He also had his bag close at hand. At three, the crew was trying different equipment in the house. Michael was trying to stay awake. It wasn't helping that the rains had started. Michael closed his eyes for a minute when Johnny called out, "We got movement!"

"Are you sure?" April asked.

"Yes, it's weird though. Movement around the back, front, and the side closest to the garage. No heat though. That's crazy," Johnny said.

Craig said, "Do you hear that?" It sounded like rakes along the sides of the house. Michael grabbed hold of his tomahawk but didn't pull it out. The scraping lasted for a few seconds, and then the power went out. The people were left in the dark. Only the fireplace was lit.

"My phone is out," April said. All the crew looked at their phones. Everyone's phone was off.

They were completely quiet as Johnny said, "Is this real? I really didn't believe we'd—"

Windows broke into the house as everyone screamed. Long branches entered the house, herding the people together in the front room. Craig called out, "Are the branches pushing us to—"

Behind the people, a window broke into the house. It was the head of the Tree Demon. Its eyes glowed as it looked around at the people. The mouth slowly dropped open as it used its branches to bring them closer. The creature called out with its cicada-like scream. Its mouth was open wide enough to fit three people. The teeth were stained with blood, and it looked hungry for more.

Michael pulled out the tomahawk and took off a horn. The creature yelled in terror. Its side branches retreated to the outside, but its head seemed stuck inside. Michael ran out the front door to attack its body while it was stuck. He turned the corner of the house to see the creature gone. Michael walked over to the hole in the house. A small light hung over him, giving him a limited view. The rain came down, and Michael was confused. How can a monster over seven feet disappear?

Michael slowly turned around and saw the creature behind him. "This is going to hurt, Michael," he heard the creature say. Michael looked at the giant tree monster. Its body extended from the house to the property's fence line. The arms spanned over twenty feet. Its limbs looked like wooden daddy longlegs.

Michael thought, I can't get by him. I can't beat him on foot. Where do I go? He looked over his shoulder and saw the open garage door. The garage looked too small for the creature to fit in. He turned and ran to the open garage. It was old. The main door opened up and out. Before he entered the garage, he tried to close the door, but it was stuck. He ran to the back, but the door was covered.

The creature slowly approached. He knew he can't get by now. "Trapped like a rat," the monster said. It bent over to peer in. They both knew that he was trapped. The creature would slowly enter the garage and feast on Michael. The rain came down, and a strike of lightning hit close. Bent over, the creature slowly approached the garage door.

A bird attacked the creature's face. Michael thought, It's the woodpecker from the statue. He can't believe this bird was trying to save him. The rain had no effect on the bird. It just flew around the creature's face, pecking as if Michael were its young. The creature flung its arms to get the bird away, but it knocked down the garage door, closing it. The creature screamed loud with its insect call as lightning crashed. The creature's branchlike arm broke through the garage door windows. Its head slammed through one of the middle windows.

Michael held his tomahawk tight when he saw the creature stuck again. Swiftly, Michael raised his tomahawk and brought it down on its head. It broke through like a wooden watermelon. The creature's head wobbled and then lowered to expose its neck. Michael got to the side and chopped its head off with three swings. The creature's body fell off the garage. Michael stood in the garage with only the light from the holes streaming in.

A few moments later, the garage door was pulled open by Craig and April. "Thanks. Where's Johnny?" Michael said.

"Oh, he quit. He jumped in his car and drove off," April said. The three of them watched as the creature's body slowly turned into ash and was washed away with the rain.

The next morning, the crew packed up their things and headed out. Michael exchanged numbers with April and Craig. "So we got nothing on that monster, no video or audio, just a couple of guys who won't sleep for a month. I think we'll do some research on it. We got a spot open if you wanna join," Craig asked.

"I can't for now. Something tells me if you keep looking for these creatures, we'll meet again," Michael said. He left the crew and headed to Mr. Blackfoot to return his tomahawk.

Michael walked outside the caretaker's cabin. He saw Patrick sitting on a log. "You waiting for me?" Michael asked.

"Yes," Patrick replied.

"I heard that the guy before didn't do so well against the drider. What happened to your buddy Milcom's guy?"

Patrick smiled and said, "That's a good story. His name was Alex. Alex found the glasses and put them right to work. All Alex ever wanted to be was a rock star. He used the glasses to make his band famous. Women, money, and drugs were his life. He wasn't a bad guy, just selfish. He loved his wife but not enough to stop the temptation of rock. Milcom had him steal ideas from other artists. Imagine working on a song and then another starts singing it. This ruined lots of singers.

"It got more serious. Milcom asked him to kill a hero. This brought him to your place in the world. He brought him to that homeless camp—the camp where you found the drider. He told him to bash the man in the blue tent with a hammer. Alex knew he would not get caught. It was just him and the homeless man. Alex asked his glasses to show him what the man did. The man was a paratrooper in Vietnam in 1969. He was a part of Operation Apache Snow in the A Sầu Valley. Many of his comrades were killed. He saved young boys over there not for medals, glory, or to be a hero. He did it because they were his brothers. He returned home to find his home didn't want him back. That man slipped in alcoholism and ended up living in a tent back in the woods.

"Alex's uncle served in Vietnam, and that memory woke him up from his selfish ways. When he refused to kill this old man, Milcom punished Alex. He took the bones out of his fingers. Alex was killed by a truck, running to what he thought was his wife."

"So now what happens?" Michael asked.

"The next moon shall be a blood moon. Then fate will bring you together. He wants your largest marble," Patrick explained.

"The masher?" Michael said.

"Yes. When you find the soldier's watch, take it. It will help you. He has not used it yet, so he doesn't know what it does. He is obsessed with the masher," Patrick said.

Michael stood up and looked around as if the answers were on the ground.

"Goodbye, Michael. I hope we will talk again." Patrick then hopped off the log and entered a door that was in a tree. The door quickly disappeared like before.

Chapter 13

THE RED MOON

Michael watched the red moon last night. He looked up at the moon with tremendous dread, knowing that tomorrow could be his last day alive. That night, he made a decision. He would always have his tools on him, the arrowhead and some stones in his pocket, marbles in the other pocket. He thought about the masher. Most of his jeans had a small pocket in front. He put the masher in that pocket. Michael thought that if this guy was so obsessed with the masher, maybe he could trick him. Days before, he got online and bought some large marbles that looked like the masher. He kept the closest-looking one with his magic marbles.

The night of the red moon, he felt like drawing a picture. He colored a red moon and a man. The man was thin and stiff. He later noticed that he didn't give the man a face. The faceless man was standing with one hand up. He wasn't afraid of the man. In fact, he felt as if the man was thanking him. He put the picture on his fridge beside a picture of him and his boy. A few days passed, and he decided to look for this guy.

Michael walked outside and instantly could smell sulfur, waste, and mildew. He looked and saw Milcom sitting on his porch swing. His glowing yellow eyes met Michael's. "Hello, Michael. I thought we'd talk for a while," the dirty little man said.

"What do you want?" Michael said.

"Well, Mr. Bond, I expect you to die." He laughed at Michael. "I just wanted you to know that you're going to lose. Man is a filthy creature.

You take and take. That's what you do. When E. skins you alive, I'll be watching." Milcom giggled.

Michael, so disgusted with this little man, told him to get off his porch. Milcom jumped off the porch swing and skipped toward the street, singing, "There goes my Mikey, movin' on down the line. Wonder where, wonder where, wonder where he is bound. I broke his heart and made him cry. Now I'm alone, so all alone. What can I do? What can I do?" He faded into nothing.

Michael walked to his car and sat inside. For a moment, he thought, Where are you going?

A second later, it felt like a bee stung him on the neck. Everything started to go fuzzy and dark. OK, no, someone behind me, he thought as he fell asleep.

Michael started to come around. He was sitting in a living room, tied up. The living room was old—old furniture, old pictures, and papers everywhere. The shag carpet made him think of his grandma's basement. The wallpaper was dirty and stained. Curtains were closed as the sun tried to break in. This gave an orange tint to the room. His bandanna was covering his mouth. Looking around the room, he saw a faceless man across from him, E.'s mannequin sitting across from him.

Feeling his pants, he noticed that his marble bag was taken. His stone bag was missing too. The arrowhead in my back pocket, he thought. He reached in his back pocket as quietly as he could. It's there. Thank god. He pulled it out and began to cut his ropes.

While he was cutting, he could hear E. in the kitchen. He was talking to himself. "What do you do? I have the marble now."

Michael kept cutting and cutting until he saw something, a watch sitting on the table. It had a green band and dried blood on the face.

Michael finally got free of his ropes on his hands. He then undid his leg ropes. With his right hand, he reached into his small pocket and found the masher. A wave of relief washed over him for a second. He then realized that E. had all his weapons. Michael slowly reached for the watch. It was an ordinary watch. It had a button on the side and dried blood from the old man he killed.

Michael examined the watch too long. He looked up and saw E. standing in the doorway with a handgun. Michael believed he was dead. This crazy man wearing a cutout mannequin's face and a dirty old thrift store suit was going to blow his head off or, worse, paralyze him. E. raised the gun to Michael. Michael, without even thinking, pushed the side button on the watch. He saw E. pull the trigger, but it looked as if he was doing it in slow motion.

Michael saw a pen falling from the table. The pen was falling slowly too. The watch slows down time, Michael realized. I can dodge the bullet and maybe live through this. The projectile left the gun in slow motion, but it was speeding up, and so was E. Michael moved out of the way of the bullet across the table. As he moved, his left leg caught the table, and he fell to the floor. While he was falling, he lost control of the masher. The big marble flew up and across the room toward the open-faced mannequin. When Michael hit the floor, time was restored to normal. E. jumped on Michael.

Michael saw the marble bounce on the rim of the mannequin's open face like the last shot in a basketball game. The marble fell into the open face of the mannequin. E. began to choke Michael. Michael can't break free of the man's gloved hands.

Michael can't breathe and saw the room going dark. E. began to laugh hysterically. Michael was about to lose consciousness when two long arms grabbed E. by the head. E. began to scream, "No, no, you can't be alive! This is my face, mine!" Dazed, Michael looked up to see the faceless mannequin holding E. by his head, his face. The mannequin buried his hands into E.'s face as if he was trying to recover it. Screams and squeals came from behind the mannequin's face until it was ripped off. The mannequin took his face. E. dropped to the floor, flopping like a fish. Michael slowly got up, never taking his eyes off the mannequin. Michael thought, Did that marble bring him to life?

Covered in blood, the mannequin slowly lifted his hand to Michael like in his picture. Michael waved back, and the mannequin fell to the floor. Michael snapped out of the trance he was in. He grabbed the watch and arrowhead. He then went to the kitchen and retrieved his bags. For a second, he thought about looking in the basement for anyone who might be trapped. Then he heard Patrick's voice. "They're all dead, son. Get out. Get out now. It's over." Michael saw his keys hanging on the key rings. He grabbed them and walked to his car that was sitting outside.

Milcom appeared over Mr. Grant's body. He kicked him and said, "Well, I guess you win. But when you think of it, I always win. People died. That's what I want."

"That's right, Michael won. Hands off."

Milcom nodded and stepped into E.'s open face. A few seconds later, the body caught on fire as both men disappeared. It didn't take long for the whole house to be engulfed by flames.

Chapter 14

New Moon

Days went by since Michael's final task. The night after, he slept for twelve hours. He woke up and put his weapons in his closet. He kept the glasses with him, knowing that Patrick would want to talk to him.

Michael went to the park and sat on his bench. He looked at the forest and thought about his journey. Not really paying attention, Michael didn't see Patrick emerge. "Hey there, boyo. How are you feeling?" Patrick asked.

"Surprisingly, I feel fine," Michael's responded.

"Good, thank you, Michael. I'm sorry you had to go through all this. On another note, you still have those gifts. You could put them away if you wish. That won't make you a bad person. Many people would. Or you could use them to help and defend those who can't. Think it over," Patrick said as he walked away.

Michael smiled and took a drink of coffee. A few seconds later, Jacob called Michael. He answered and talked to his boy. Jacob was coming to stay with his dad for a while. They both missed each other.

PART 2

Chapter 15

A NEW START

The summer after Michael's ordeal of terror, he took some time off with his boy. Jacob was with him for the summer. They went to Florida for vacation. Michael and his ex had a better relationship since. He would get the boy on the summer break for six weeks. This would give Jacob and his mom a break. Jacob and his dad could get together and reconnect.

On the beach in Daytona, Michael thought long and hard about the choice he would have to make. How would he support himself if he went around chasing monsters? Would his son be safe from the monsters? How would he feel letting monsters run free?

Sitting on the beach, his phone rang. It was Craig from the TV show he helped with. "Hey, Michael, how's it going?" Craig asked.

Michael told him that he was on the beach. "So make it quick." Craig told Michael that there was an opening on their crew. Johnny never came back, and Michael seemed to fit in. The job would take him around the country looking for haunted houses and monsters. They would be free during the late spring and summer months. Michael thanked Craig for the job offer and told him he would let him know when he got back home from vacation.

Michael made the decision before they came home. He told Jacob that he had a new job on TV. This excited Jacob and asked if he'd be on

TV. Michael laughed and told him he was going to be a technical adviser. They had a great time in Florida, and Michael wished it would never end. All good things come to an end. Soon Jacob would go back to his mom and to school. Michael would start a new job and use his new gifts to make the world a little safer from things that go bump in the night.

Chapter 16

BUSHWHACKER WOODS BEAST

Michael got out of the car and looked around. He'd never been to Hermann, Missouri. He was aware of the Oktoberfest they had every year but not of any haunted cabins. The crew checked into the motel, and they agreed to meet up for dinner at seven. Michael went to his room, set an alarm, and went to sleep. When he woke up, he cleaned up and headed to Craig's room.

Craig had a book for Michael. He handed him an old journal. "This is a journal from a soldier in the Civil War. He was a bushwhacker out of Missouri. He's the main guy we are focusing on. His story is pretty good but kind of unbelievable," Craig said.

Michael looked at the journal and shook his head. The crew headed toward dinner, and Michael began to read the journal. It didn't look like the original manuscript. Michael opened it, and he could tell it was photocopied. The copies looked real enough. Michael guessed that the owner did not want it in the hands of TV people. He didn't blame the owner.

August 28, 1861

My dearest Mary,

I am writing in this journal for a number of reasons. It keeps my mind on you. I will continue to write you letters. This journal is in case they never make it to you. My best friend, Thomas, said he would deliver this to you if I meet my fate. In turn, I have been writing letters for Thomas to send home to his mother. We have been walking a long way. I don't think I've ever walked so far in my life. I fear that we will meet our foes soon, but I am no coward. I am resolved to the cause. Thank you for the picture you gave me. It brightens my days and nights to see you. My commanding officers are hollering at us to get up and move on. Till my next rest.

Jefferson

September 3, 1861

My dearest Mary,

Yesterday was my first battle. I don't ever remember being so scared in my entire life. At the time of the battle, I just kept shooting and reloading. I am pleased to say that I did not sustain any physical injuries and do not wish to write what I saw. I only hope this terrible thing will be over soon.

Yours truest,

Jefferson

Michael thumbed through the journal, reading the point of view of this young stranger, getting to know him more with every entry. He put the journal away to eat dinner with the cast. They were excited about this case. The cabin was miles to the south. At first light, they would head out.

Michael went back to him room and finished reading the journal. The strangest part was the last few entries.

July 7, 1865

My Mary,

I don't know why I'm still writing in this journal. I came home to find you have succumbed to fever. The Yankees are to blame for this and those damn redlegs. I am writing this down because it does not feel real. Yesterday I was sitting on the side of our lake. All I could think of was revenge. If only I could hurt the people responsible for taking my beloved. I sat there, and the hate just grew.

I looked behind me, and I saw a man. He was dressed in a fancy suit, like he was an actor on a stag. I asked him what he was doing behind me. He just smiled with a grin that seemed to wrap around his whole face. The man stunk like burnt animal hide and sulfur. He said that he was a friend of the Confederacy. I told him that there was no more Confederacy. He just gave me that giant smile with teeth so big I thought he could eat me. He said that if I wanted to, I could have a lifetime of vengeance. All I had to do was sign this piece of paper. The paper would allow me to kill Yankees and never get caught by a Yankee. I didn't believe him, so I signed it to get him away. I signed my dead friend Thomas's name.

The man began to laugh at me. He said, "Jefferson, Thomas died two years ago." At that point, I knew he was the devil. He showed me the signature I wrote down, and it was mine. The devil laughed at me. He told me that my deal would be three nights a month. Since one of my favorite books was The Man-Wolf, I would turn into a wolf on the full moon and two days after. He said that to guarantee that I kill Yankees, after those, I'd see you again until the next moon. Tonight is the first full moon. I suspect I'll see you soon.

Eternally yours,

Jefferson

September 5

Mary,

Tonight is the full moon. I have seen you the last two months. I feel no regret, and I hope those Yankees suffered at my hands. I will see you soon.

Jefferson

July 14, 1897

Mary,

It has been three months since I have seen you. A pain in me has grown. I no longer wish to kill. I have since chained myself underground to keep from feeding. Something different about me. I have not grown older since that day I met the man by the lake. I feel as if I will live forever. If this is my curse, I pray no one ever finds me when I change. I'm not as strong as I hoped to be. Regretfully, I know I will see you again.

Jefferson

Michael put down the journal and put on his glasses. He immediately saw the cabin. It was sitting in a clearing and looked welcoming. Just as he thought that, blood came from in between the logs and from the windows. Michael heard an animal-like creature breathing on his neck. The hot breath scared him almost as much as when he felt the creature lick him. Michael instantly knew they were in trouble.

The next morning, the crew met in front of the motel to check their supplies. Michael was standing outside, looking at the lush green trees. He looked over at the gas station, debating on whether to get an energy drink. Looking at the station with his glasses on, he thought, *What is* that guy wearing? The young man was wearing an old brown shirt and trousers. He had an old pair of boots on that had seen better days. The young man looked like a Civil War reenactor without the gray uniform. Michael tilted his glasses down and saw the man was wearing a gas station service attendant uniform.

A thought instantly went through Michael's mind. This was the man from the journal he just read. Michael walked over to the station and started a conversation with the young man. "Hello, how's your day?" Michael said.

"It ain't raining, so that's a start," the young man said. They both laughed and talked. "What are you folks doing in my fair town?"

"We're doing a television show. We are going to a cabin in the woods a few miles to the south. Do you know it?" Michael asked.

The young man nodded.

"We are going to document the life of the family who lived there. We'll be very respectful," Michael said.

"I hope you are. I will give you a little advice. If you plan to stay there overnight, I would not venture off the property. The woods aren't a good place to run around at night, lots of wild animals," the young man said with a smile.

Michael thanked the young man and walked away. He gave the journal back to Craig. "You sure you want to do this?" Michael asked.

Craig smiled and said, "Well, I am now. Thank god I got silver bullets in my .357." He then brandished a silver revolver. The crew jumped into the vehicles and headed to the cabin. As they drove off, Michael saw the young man wave goodbye.

On the way out there, Craig and April started recording their journey to the cabin. They took many takes of the backstory. They cited excerpts from the journal. Upon their arrival, the cabin looked like a museum piece from Frontierland. Inside the cabin was more of the same. There were a table and chairs with mannequins sitting at it. Michael looked at the mannequins, and a chill went up his spine. A note on the table read, "These clothes are from the original residence." The lady mannequin had a bonnet that caught Michael's eye. His glasses seemed to focus on that.

Michael went outside and sat on a rocking chair. He asked the glasses to tell him the story of this place. The glasses went dark, and then he could see.

There wasn't much modern technology around the cabin when he asked the glasses, but the few things there disappeared. Michael could see a group of people standing around an open grave. This must have been Mary's funeral. The people from the past looked sad. A priest was standing in front of the people, reading from the Bible. With the glasses on, Michael could hear the crying people and smell a fire somewhere. He was always amazed to see what the glasses let him see with all his senses, the smells and sounds in the background mostly.

During the ceremony, the priest walked around the grounds of the property. It looked as if he was blessing it. An older man asked the priest what he was doing. The priest said that Mary asked him to consecrate the grounds. Michael watched as the priest blessed the grounds around the cabin. He noticed that he blessed everything that was in the fence line of the cabin.

The scene changed, and he saw the young man from the gas station. He ran up the walkway to Mary's grave. The man fell to his knees, weeping uncontrollably at her grave. Michael remembered losing friends and feeling the same way that young man did. He almost felt wrong watching this private moment of loss.

The scene changed again. Michael watched Mary walk out of the house and start to do chores. She went to the garden and swept the front porch. He looked down the road and saw the young man running up to see her. The man crossed over the threshold to the property, and the woman disappeared. He looked confused and hurt. The man called her name and ran inside the cabin. Angry, he walked off the property and started down the road. Once he exited the property, the woman reappeared.

The man disappeared, and the landscape changed. It was as if he was watching time-lapse photography on the property. She called out to him. He turned around and went to hold her. She stopped at the property's edge. He again went to hold her, and she disappeared when he walked on the property. The man screamed out in pain. He took a deep breath and slowly took a step back just over the property line. His lady love reappeared. Carefully, he reached over to hold her, making sure his feet stood off the property. To his luck, she did not disappear, and they were able to embrace.

Michael then saw a series of times where the man would meet his lady at that same spot. The seasons would change, but they would meet regardless of the weather. The series of meetings stopped at a moment where they seemed to be at an argument. The man, Jefferson, was telling her that he was sorry. Michael realized that he had told her what he'd been doing. Mary cried and told him that he needed to stop. She then walked off the property and disappeared.

A series of seasons changed and no reunion of the couple. Michael watched this until Jefferson walked up slowly. He was dressed in more modern clothes, closer to the 1950s. Michael saw Mary walk out of the cabin. She acted as if the argument never happened. Jefferson saw this and smiled.

The glasses turned dark. Michael saw that it was nighttime at the cabin. Nighttime in the woods was dark. The property had changed from when Michael first started watching. A new building had appeared on the property. A single line from the road ran into it. Michael knew it was the generator building. He remembered from the show's background report. The county added a generator building a few years after they declared the property a county historic site back in the 1970s. The property had a few light posts that kept the grounds somewhat lit. Michael could hear crickets calling out.

The calm scene was broken by a bloodcurdling scream. Michael saw three people running up the road. The road had been widened over the years. It was about twenty yards wide from tree line to tree line. A woman and two men were running for their lives. One of the men was falling behind the two. The man and the woman yelled at him to come on. They both looked at him when something from the woods jumped out and took him back into the darkness. The creature was the size of a grizzly bear. It moved with the speed of a cat. They both froze as tree limbs exploded and landed on the road.

With disbelief, they began to run toward the cabin again. They made it to the cabin, and they both were hysterical. The man and woman looked around the cabin for a phone. They couldn't find one, so the man grabbed an ax that was by the fireplace. The lady looked out the window and kept saying, "It took him." The man told her they would wait here for a while. He said if it didn't come back, they would make their way to the river.

They slowly walked out of the cabin toward the generator building. The man was just about to the door when the creature threw their friend's arm at them. The arm had been ripped off. Both of them screamed and ran into the woods. A few moments later, Michael heard a loud howling from where they ran to. Michael also saw a coyote grab the arm and disappear with it into the woods.

Michael sat there looking at the dark road. He was waiting for the glasses to change, but they didn't. A few seconds later, he saw it. It walked up the road slowly. With every breath it took, a snarl came too. The creature stopped at the property's edge and stood up. It stood over eight feet in the air. Its glowing wolf's eyes stared at Michael.

Michael stood up and walked to the other side of the porch. The eyes felt too intense. He got to the other side, and the beast was still staring at him. Michael moved a couple of times, and the beast kept his eyes on him. The beast could see Michael, and they both knew it. It then raised its head to the sky and gave a tremendous howl. Michael could feel the howl on his whole body. It caused him to cover his ears and close his eyes.

Michael opened his eyes, and the beast was gone. He could see it was daylight, and he saw Jefferson walking up the road. Jefferson was about a football field away from the point where they would meet. Michael turned to the door and saw Mary staring at him. She said, "Michael, if you're going to be here, don't leave the grounds." Michael was shocked that she was talking to him.

"Can he be saved?" Michael asked.

"He lost his soul lifetimes ago. I'm just a shadow of the life we shared, an echo of Mary. Mary has moved on to another life. One day the devil will collect him. He always does," Mary said.

The glasses started to fade back to normal. Michael could hear Mary say, "Stay on the property."

Michael sat in the rocking chair as the crew moved around. Craig and April came out of the cabin laughing. April looked at the road and said, "Thank god they're here." A truck pulled up with two young people. Michael asked Craig what was going on.

"We are going to have two kids run through the woods over there, not deep in the woods or at night. They will reenact a missing person story that happened out here. Why, are you getting spooked?" Craig said.

"As long as we stay on the property at night, no wandering in the woods. I think that would be safer for everyone," Michael said.

Craig knew that Michael wasn't trying to run the show. He was trying to keep everyone safe. Craig smiled and nodded in agreement.

The day went on with the crew filming the two young people in the woods. They were reenacting the missing people whom Michael had seen earlier. Michael heard the young girl scream from the woods. He could tell she was acting. It didn't sound anything like what he heard earlier. The crew had some dinner on picnic tables on the property. The two young people left before nightfall. They were local to the area and didn't want to be there after dark.

The crew set up their equipment for the ghost hunting. Michael took his post, making sure the computers didn't fail. Darkness fell, and the TV show started. Craig and April used their night vision to walk around and talk to the spirits. One of the cast members went outside and made scratching noises. Throughout the night, they filmed and reviewed the footage.

At around three, they all sat round the computer, looking at their recordings. They were trying to decide if they needed anything else. A large howl came from the far woods. Everyone stopped. April said, "Record, record." Craig and April went outside on the porch and listened to the silence. Nothing came from the woods, nothing whatsoever, no frogs, crickets, or cicadas. It was stone quiet.

Then a large howl came again, but this time, it was just outside the wooden fence of the property. Craig said, "Either there are two of these things or whatever made that noise is very fast."

April said, "Someone bring me the thermal." They could both hear something walk along the perimeter. It was just far back enough, so they couldn't see it. April pointed the thermal imager toward the woods. For a second, she saw a heat signature of an animal as large as a bear.

"Look! Did you see that?" April cried. The cameraman was too slow to catch it. A moment later, they heard the howl again coming from far away. They stood on the porch for an hour with no more noises from the woods.

Craig turned to go back inside when he was startled. The female mannequin was looking right at him. Michael had stood the mannequin up and put her in the window. For a second, Craig thought that Michael had done that to make whatever was out there go away.

The next morning, the crew wrapped up their duties. April said that they had what they came for. Michael walked around the grounds, looking around. He went to Mary's grave. He pulled out a crayon from his special supply. Michael colored a little heart on the grave and said a private prayer. An hour later, they jumped into their cars and headed back. Michael looked back as they drove down the road and saw Mary waving goodbye from the porch.

Chapter 17

THE NIGHT KNOCK-KNOCKERS

Craig, April, and Michael decided to drive together to the next spot on their Scare Crew adventure. April passed a folder to Michael and told him that this was the next place that they were going. "We are headed to a little town just west of Kansas City. We are headed to the home of Jessica Rae. Jessica was one of my favorite authors when I was a little girl. I have read her books and stories about her life," April said to Michael.

"Well, since this is going to be a long drive, please tell me her story. I would love to hear it from a fan," Michael said with great enthusiasm. They all laughed, and April agreed to tell the backstory to Jessica Rae.

"Jessica Rae was a famous author out of Kansas. She wrote a series of four books about supernatural boogeymen. The series was the Night Knock-Knockers. I believe, in the book, she said that Reggie got cut on his ears or face. It was something that required Reggie to spend the night with the vet. The boys had a restless night without their dog," April said, looking deep into Michael's eyes.

"Every child will tell you that when you turn off the lights in your room, the pile of clothes turn into a large old gray man with eyes constantly staring at you. The ten-year-old said that he saw the shadow of multiple figures on his wall and dresser. When he turned the light on, they disappeared. He did this a couple of times until the twelve-year-old told him to cut it out. The younger brother told him what was scaring him and asked him to stay awake to see if he saw it too.

"The lights went out, and both boys saw nothing but darkness. After their eyes adjusted to the darkness, the elder brother turned on the lights. He said that he thought he saw something too. The boys moved clothes and items to lessen the fear in their hearts. They turned the lights off again, and they saw nothing again. Their eyes adjusted again, and they continued to see nothing. Relief washed over them, and they both tried to fall asleep until they heard a knock.

"It was as if someone knocked their knuckles on the dresser twice. Knock, knock. The younger brother asked if his big brother made that noise. With a whimper, the elder brother said no. Another knock-knock came from the wall by the closet door. The knocks came slowly with half a second between them. A few seconds later, another set of knocks came from the other side of the room as if they were answering each other. The younger brother, almost crying, asked his big brother what they should do.

"There was a knock-knock from the footboard of the younger brother's bed. The elder brother reached for the light but then stopped. He then knocked twice on the dresser that held the lamp. For a minute, all was quiet. Suddenly, there was a continuous knock from one spot in the room and then two spots, five spots until it felt like the knocks were closing in on them and speeding up as they got closer. The elder brother turned on the light, and nothing was there.

"Three days later, their father was passing their room and saw that the boys had fallen asleep with the lights on. This time, Reggie was already back and asleep on the floor between the boys. The dad turned off the light, and he heard Reggie start to growl. He told the dog to cut it out. 'It's me, Reggie.' He shut the door and heard a knock from inside the boys' room. The dad opened the door, and the light was on. Both boys were sitting up awake, and Reggie looked ready to pounce. The dad asked what was going on in there. The boys told their father the story of the knocking. He told them that they had nothing to be afraid of.

"The boys told the father to come into their room and turn off the lights. They would step outside and let him experience the knocking by himself so he didn't think it was the boys making the noise. The father agreed to do it, and the boys left the room. Reggie left the room with his boys. He sat on one of the boys' bed and reached for the light. A little fear crept into his heart. He turned the light out, and nothing happened. After a minute, the dad reached for the light and heard a knock-knock. He paused for a minute and then heard another knock-knock. The dad turned on the light and saw nothing. He turned off the light and waited for the knocking to continue. A minute later, he heard the knock-knock again. The dad knocked back hard. Ten seconds later, the room was filled with fast knocking—knocking from the dressers, doors, walls, and floor by his feet. He turned on the light. For an instant, like a single frame in a movie, he saw dozens of shadow figures closing in on him. The family did not stay a single night in that house after that.

"Jessica tracked down the family who used to live there. She talked the father into telling his story. He said that he would deny what he told her. The father told her about the events that happened. He also told her to get a dog. When the dog was in the house, nothing happened. Jessica loved the story. She told him she was a writer, and she was going to use the story. The father said, 'Lose my information, and I don't want a penny.' We tried to get a hold of him, but we couldn't find him. Jessica is the main story anyways. After her fourth book about the Night Knock-Knockers, she disappeared along with the caretaker of the house," April said.

"Caretaker?" Michael questioned.

"Yes, the caretaker. After book 1, she moved out of the house and lived in New York for a while. The house was donated to the town as a historic house. With her book money, she bought furniture from the period that the house was built. A retired librarian watched over the residence. One night after book number 4 came out, they both went bye-bye. Police conducted an investigation with no leads. A new caretaker took over. They have tours in the house and historic cooking classes. No one stays there at night. Only on Halloween does the caretaker pass out candy. She stays outside most of the time. The school district uses the house for summer school. That school district has the lowest summer school attendance in the state. The kids scare themselves out of that house." April laughed.

Michael smiled and said, "If the dad thinks a dog is a good idea, maybe Nick can get with the police K9 in town, maybe offer some off-duty work, just in case." Craig agreed with Michael. April gave Michael the first book in the series that Jessica wrote. Michael sat back and started to read the book.

The crew pulled up to the house and began to unload TV equipment. Michael looked around at the house and the neighborhood. The houses were old and well kept. Lawns were mowed and gardens still in bloom. The house they were going to was amazing. It was two stories, blue, and Victorian-style and had a wraparound porch. Michael hoped that no "spiders" lived under there.

Michael looked up the history of the town and the house. The town was established in the early 1800s as a European trading post. The residence was built in the early 1900s. The first owner was a wealthy landowner. It stayed with the family until a series of tragedies at the start of the 1960s. The owner of the time hung himself after his wife ran away with another man. The son who inherited the house went missing during the 1970s. He left no notes for why he left. Family member fought over control over the house. In the 1980s, a great-grandson took possession of the residence. Rumor has it that he was scared of the property. He put it on the market. None of the remaining family members wanted the house. The house ended up in the hands of the family before Jessica Rae.

Michael felt he was caught up on the house. Craig called Michael and April over to go over the plan for the house. "We are going to do some interviews with locals around the house to get some history. While we are doing that, the crew will record the Jessica Rae reenactors. We'll have dinner, and then we'll set up for the night watch. Nick got a hold of the K9 unit in town. He's going to stay the night with us just in case the legends are true," Craig said with a smile.

Craig and April grabbed some cameras and started walking around the neighborhood. Michael went inside and helped set up the ghost-catching devices. When he was done, Michael sat on the porch. The night was a calm cool fall afternoon. Michael pulled his glasses down and asked, "What happened to Jessica Rae?"

A lady walked into the house with a box in her hands. The room was empty, and today was moving-in day. She looked around the living room and seemed satisfied. This was Jessica Rae's new place. She put the box down and used it to keep the door open. Four large men carrying boxes followed inside and put the boxes down marked "Living room." She thanked them as they walked outside to get more stuff from the truck.

Looking around, she talked to herself. She kept telling herself, "This is the place." This was the place where she'd write her novel and become famous. She'd donate the house to the town and become a legend. Her fans would travel far and wide to come here. Here was where it all started, and here was where she made her name. Jessica felt extremely lucky to get the house. The house came with history, bad history. That was part of the reason she bought it. She hoped the negative history would help her on her horror novel. If she only knew how right she was.

The first week, she got settled into the house. She met the neighbors and put her things away. A week or two later, a letter came for the former residents. She was curious about them. Jessica knew it was a family of four. They were eager to sell, and they had unwelcome visitors. Jessica had a friend in the police department and had her look up the residents. The family had moved on the other side of the metro. Both towns were on the outer parts of the metro. One was on the far east, and the other was west. She decided to pay the family a visit and maybe talk to one of the adults about the house. The mail was her excuse to speak.

Later that week, she drove forty minutes to reach the quiet neighborhood that the family moved to. Jessica knocked on the door, and a man answered. He seemed pleasant enough. Jessica introduced herself, handed the mail, and asked about her new house. The man' s demeanor changed instantly. He wasn't angry, but he was scared, the kind of scared a person who doesn't want to be found gives when they are found. He closed the door behind him and told her the story of the Night Knock-Knockers. After the story, Jessica didn't quite believe him, but she believed that he wasn't lying. Everything he said he believed.

Jessica asked the man if she could use his story for a book she was writing. The man said that she could use it if she never mentioned his family, his family never profited from it, and she never contacted him again. Jessica agreed to the terms. He also told her to get a dog. The only time bad stuff happened in that house was when a dog was not there. He said, "As soon as you knock back, a dog will keep the knocks away from that room and that room only." He found that out when they were moving out.

During the time when the family was moving their stuff, the dad went back to help the moving company. The company requested him to be there. He took Reggie with him. The dad used the bathroom alone, and he realized it was a mistake. He went to pee and moved his hand to the toilet handle. Before he could flush it, he heard a knock-knock. It came from inside the toilet bowl water reservoir. He was frozen with fear. Before he could move, a knock came from the medicine cabinet mirror. The knock sounded like someone was behind the mirror, trying to get out. He walked to the door as carefully as he could, but a knock came from the door. Trapped in the bathroom, he finally zipped up himself. He turned quickly to hear the knock-knock from the bathroom window. The bathroom was on the second floor, so his fear was almost out of control. Just before he was about to scream, he heard Reggie bark at the door. The dad instantly opened the door to see his dog looking at him. He said that Reggie looked at him like he was a big dummy.

Jessica shook the man's hand and said goodbye. He told her before she left that he didn't need any mail from there again. She smiled, thanked him, and drove away. Jessica went straight to the county pound and got a rescue. That year, she and her dog, Otis, wrote the first of four books she would write.

Michael watched as her house changed from modest to elegant. The furniture she bought for the house was early-1930s-style. Then there was a ceremony on the front porch. The mayor of the town and Jessica were standing together. He said, "I want to thank Miss Rae for donating her beautiful home to our historical society. This will not be just a museum, but Miss Cathy will conduct historical classes and events here." A lady in the crowd waved her hand to the people.

The house became a living museum. During the summer, kids would do crafts in the backyard. In the kitchen, Miss Cathy (the caretaker) conducted cooking classes. The living room looked like a small library. It had plenty of Jessica Rae's best sellers. Michael then saw Jessica and Miss Cathy sitting in the porch. Jessica said to her, "I think this is going to be my last Knockers book. I'm ready to write about something else."

Miss Cathy looked shocked. "Why? Everyone loves that series," she said.

"Nope, it's time. I'm going to stop the Knockers so I won't fall back on them," Jessica said as she looked into the sky.

Michael then saw Jessica packing her bags at a hotel she was staying at. It seemed that time passed from the talk on the porch. The phone rang. Jessica answered it and looked annoyed. "Yes, Miss Cathy," she said. She listened quietly until the person on the other end was done. "OK, I'll come by on my way out." She didn't want to swing by, but she knew she had to.

Jessica pulled up to the house at about noon. When she got out and looked around, she noticed that no one was around. That was strange to her. The street wasn't busy, but there was always someone cutting grass or sitting on their porch. She walked in and called out to Miss Cathy. Miss Cathy called back and said that she was in the basement. Jessica walked down the stairs to see a chair sitting in the middle of the basement. There was a sharp pain to the back of her head, and lights went out.

Jessica woke up hours later with a splitting headache. Her hands were tied behind her back. She was tied to the chair, and her mouth was covered with cloth. From where she was sitting in the basement, she was able to see up the stairs into the kitchen. The kitchen lights were on, and it was nighttime now. She saw Miss Cathy walk through the kitchen and down the basement stairs. "Well, I'm glad you're awake. For a second, I thought I killed you," Miss Cathy said.

Jessica tried to talk but couldn't.

"Now, now you talk too much. This is the part were the evil genius tells you her plan. You see, my family used to own this property. You didn't know that because I took my husband's name. Before I could get it back, you scooped it up. While this house sat empty because my family squabbled over it, I took care of it. I cleaned up this crappy little town. Homeless people, drug dealers, and whores all used this very basement. They came down here. The knock-knockers did their job. The more the children talked about this house being a boogeyman house, the stronger they got—until that family moved in. They went quiet. I even broke in to try to wake them up. That dog they had—they are afraid of dogs if you can believe that, not just any dogs but the love kids have with dogs. They are the ultimate defense against these things that go knock in the night."

Miss Cathy laughed. "This is what's going to happen. You killed them in your book, so they are returning the favor. When you're gone without a trace, their power will increase again, this time nationwide."

Miss Cathy put a rolling pin on Jessica's lap. "You're going to be here in the dark. I know you're smart, and you won't knock back. That's OK. Eventually, that rolling pin will fall, and that will sound like a knock-knock to me," Miss Cathy said as she walked up the stairs.

At the top of the stairs, she turned off the lights and closed the door. Everything went black. Jessica could only see the light coming from under the kitchen door up the stairs. She struggled to get free when she heard it. Knock, knock. Jessica was frozen with fear. The sound can't come from across the room. Then there was a knock-knock from behind her against the wall. At the same time, she heard a knock-knock from the floor in front of her and on the ceiling. She was frozen with fear. All she could do was think about the rolling pin. Don't let it hit, she thought.

A few moments later, she felt an icy hand roll across her jeans and grasp the pin. Jessica could hear the creature pat the pin as if it were a baby needing to be burped. Then she heard the rolling pin hit the floor. Knock, knock, knock, knock. Miss Cathy was right; it did sound like a knock. Over Jessica's right shoulder, she felt as if someone's face was over it. The breath was cold and rotten. The thing beside her let out a tremendous scream. The high-pitched scream sounded like a wild animal caught in a trap—a trap that was eating it alive. Then all was quiet.

The kitchen door flew open after what seemed forever. Miss Cathy said, "Goodbye, Miss Jess—" Miss Cathy was shocked to see her. "You're not supposed to be here. They took you. I heard the cry!" She stood at the top of the stairs in disbelief.

Jessica could see the lights behind Miss Cathy going out. Miss Cathy turned around and saw the lights go dark. "What's going on?" she said. In the blackness of the kitchen, the knocking began. "No, no, I brought her to you. I serve you!" The knocking kept speeding up while Miss Cathy kept shouting no. Jessica saw Miss Cathy getting pulled into the darkness with a scream that instantly stopped.

Jessica sat in the basement, trying to get free, when she heard the knocking again coming from the dark kitchen. She looked up in the kitchen when the basement lights went out. The lights came on a few seconds later, and Jessica was gone.

Michael could see the neighborhood in real time now. He reached up to pull his glasses off to reflect on the story he saw. He pulled, and the glasses wouldn't come off. Something was holding them on. The Night Knock-Knockers wanted him to see one more thing.

Three young boys rode up to the house on their bikes. "OK, Grant, I dared you to do it. You said you weren't scared," one boy said to another.

"I ain't scared of anything." There brave boy walked up the stairs and knocked on the door. He shouted to his friends' count.

The two other boys said, "One, two, three, won't take me. Four, five, still alive. Six, seven, won't see heaven. Eight, nine, ten, knock, knock again."

The visibly frightened boy knocked twice and waited. The boy blew out a deep breath and turned to his friends. "See, I—" The door exploded with dozens of knocks coming from the inside. It was too many knocks to be real, like fifty pairs of fists quickly knocking. The boy flew off the porch. Michael could swear that the boy's feet never touched the ground.

The force that was holding the glasses relaxed. Michael realized that this entity wanted people's fear. Tonight they would get a show. Their show, Scare Crew, was on TV, and people would be scared of whatever they filmed tonight but not enough to think it was real. It would be scary enough to keep the lights on though.

Craig and April returned from their neighborhood tour. April had that hungry look in her eyes. The rest of the crew came on the porch. Two of the crew left to get dinner. Michael remained on the porch.

After dinner, a police car pulled up. A tall bald officer stepped out of the car. He opened the back door for his partner. A Belgian shepherd stepped out. The dog looked around and walked over to a tree to relieve himself. After his doggy business, he came out to the porch. "Hi, everyone. I'm Mark, and this is Ike," the officer said. Ike sat on the porch, looking at everyone. Craig shook the cop's hand and told him where he would be.

Michael sat at his station, with Nick and Mark sitting beside him. Throughout the night, April and Craig went every room, talking, knocking, and staying completely quiet. Nothing happened for most of the night. Craig had no idea why. April was the most disappointed out of everyone. At about three, Craig asked Michael if he had any ideas. Craig didn't want to have the crew knock off camera, but he was prepared to save this episode. Michael said, "The lights need to be off, Craig."

Craig replied, "They are. They've been off all night."

Michael calmly said, "Turn off the night vision."

Craig smiled and said, "OK."

Craig and April went to the boy's room and started. They turned off the night vision. Michael could only pick up audio from the monitors. A few moments later, Ike began to growl. Mark told him to cut it out. In the room where April and Craig were, nothing was happening. Craig began to ask if anyone was there when a knock-knock happened. They both asked, "Was that you?" There was a knock-knock again.

Craig said, "I'm going to knock back." The room went quiet for a minute. Then the room erupted with knocks all over the surfaces of the room. Craig called out for lights. The lights came on, and there was nothing.

April said, "Let's do that again." As soon as the lights went out, a high-pitched scream came from the room. Michael recognized the scream from watching Jessica's story, the animal-caught-in-a-trap scream. The lights came back on. Craig and April were white as ghost. After a while, they tried again, but the noises were gone.

The next morning, Craig told Michael that was a good call. Michael asked if they would believe that was real. Craig said, "I think they will, but they'll say it was fake so they can sleep at night." Michael told Craig he could live the rest of his life and never hear that scream again. That would be OK.

Chapter 18

Fifteen Minutes of Fame

Standing at the tree line at Michael's hometown park, Daryl and Kyle used their selfie stick. "Hey there, everyone. This is KD Adventures. I'm the Kyle, coming at you live," Kyle said.

"Hi, I'm Daryl, and this is episode 'Midwest.' This is the midwestern town we are doing. If you guess correct, you'll be put in a drawing to be on one of our shows next year." Both young men swung their cameras around. They did three more takes and turned off their cameras.

Daryl looked at Kyle and said, "OK, dude. If we get in there and our GPS fails, we turn around." Kyle nodded as he checked his supplies.

Both men walked into the woods, ready to record their internet show. The men had a popular web show where they walked in large woods/forest and display how to survive. This was from a young person's point of view. They selected this site because of the large number of missing persons in the area.

An hour into the trek, Daryl set up a scene. "OK, we are lost in the woods. Remember to stay calm. What do I do? We will show you some things," Kyle said. Daryl looked at his GPS, and it showed to be working. He looked at the device and saw where he marked the point where they would have to walk to. They would spend the night in the woods and slowly make their way to the meet-up point. If they were late, the people looking for them would just follow the GPS signal.

Most of the day, they would walk and talk to the camera. They stopped for lunch by a creek. Kyle mentioned that he hadn't seen deer, nothing larger than a squirrel. Just before dark, they found a small clearing. They both decided that this was a good place for a campsite. A small fire was started, and they cooked their dinner. "These woods don't feel right," Kyle said.

"I know what you mean, dude," Daryl agreed.

"It feels like something is watching us," Kyle said.

They didn't believe in guns; both men had hunting knives on them. Daryl decided to demonstrate how to make spears. This kept the fear out of their minds. They didn't know why they were uneasy. This was not their first show. Two shows ago, a wolf walked by their tent. Daryl had bear spray and his trusty hunting knife. The wolf walked by and sniffed around. It left after a while. That was scary to them, but it was mostly exciting. This was a different feeling.

"Let's go sleep, and we'll get this one over with," Daryl said. Both men went into their tent. They went to sleep uneasy and on guard.

Daryl woke up confused and unable to move. He tried to call for help, but his mouth was covered with a sticky substance. He was being dragged through the woods. It wasn't daylight yet. The woods were still dark, but it was getting lighter. He could barely see Kyle next to him being dragged too. Kyle was out. It looked as if he was bleeding from the head. His body was wrapped into a cocoon. Daryl struggled to get free and see what was dragging him. He could hear numerous legs pulling him. Just as he was about to see what this thing was, they were pulled into a cave.

Blackness washed over him. Daryl felt himself being pulled by his feet. He was being hung by his feet. Whatever had them stunk. Daryl can hear feet tapping around him. He thought, What is this? Am I asleep, and is Kyle dead?

A bright light came on ten feet from him. His GPS light brightened the cave. Daryl was in disbelief. Two giant creatures were standing in front of him. Their bodies were of giant spiders with long hairy black legs. They both had bloated abdomens. Coming from where the spider head was supposed to be was a man's torso. It was white and looked like a corpse. Their heads were black and hairy. They had red eyes the size of plums. One of the creatures was holding a deer by its neck. The deer was alive but not fighting. It looked just as scared as Daryl.

Daryl looked around the cave and saw at least four people hung up like him. The people were dead. Their guts and rib cages looked like something broke out of them. They were missing heads and limbs too.

Daryl looked at the creature holding the GPS. He thought, It's nothing. Just leave it.

In Daryl's mind, he heard, Then they'll find us, Daryl. We're not ready for that yet. He locked eyes with the creature. It put the GPS onto the side of the deer and used webbings to stick it onto its side. The other creature let go, and the deer ran out of the cave. This left Daryl in darkness again. Daryl tried to scream but couldn't as the creatures ate him alive.

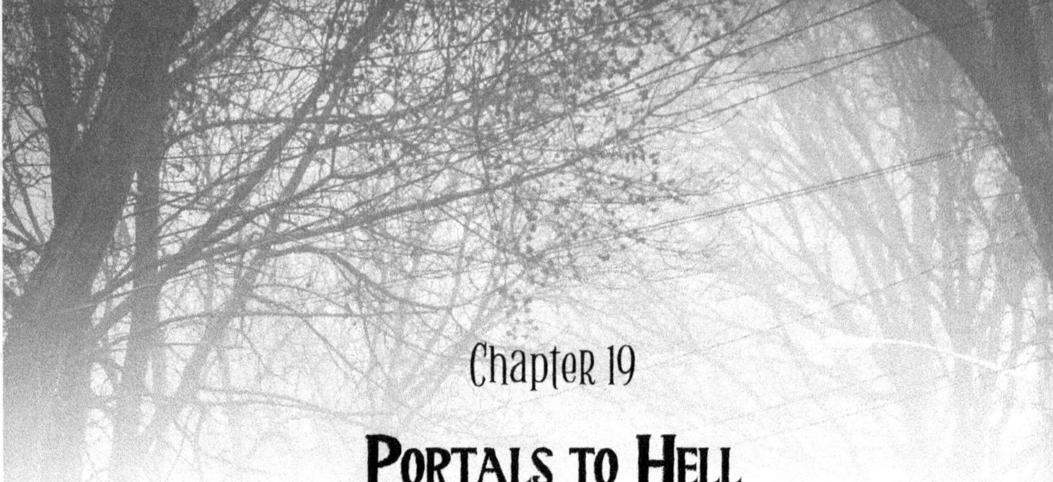

Chapter 19

PORTALS TO HELL

Michael was riding in the back of the car, with Craig driving and April riding shotgun. April smiled and said to Michael, "OK, this is our plans for this week. Since we are in Kansas, we are going to the Hell Tour around Kansas."

Michael smiled and questioned, "Hell Tour?"

"In Stull, Kansas, is reported to be a portal to hell. Most people say that a person made it up for a paper. We will find out. After the cemetery, we will drop you off in your hometown so you can check your house out and do whatever you need to do. When you're done, just hop on a plane and catch up with Craig and me. We are going to drive straight through to our next stop in Iowa," April said.

Michael watched as April put in her earbuds and take a long drink off her coffee. Craig had his earpiece in, and he was talking to someone on the phone. Michael sat back and thought about a portal to hell. He said out loud to himself, "I wonder what a portal to hell would look like."

A large gust of wind rocked the car for a second. This wind made Michael realize that he had his special glasses on. He thought, What if the glasses show me a real portal to hell?

Before he could pull them off, he saw a minivan pull alongside their car. The parents in the front looked tired of the kids in the back. They had a baby in a child seat. In the back row, two kids were on their tablets. Even on their tablets, they looked loud. Michael saw a thin man who was bent over in the middle seat by the baby. The man was in a formal suit. His hair was black and slicked back with oil. He looked in on the baby with his long, thin fingers. The family looked as if they didn't even notice him in the van, looking at the baby with a smile that seemed to wrap around his face.

Slowly, he raised his eyes to Michael. His mouth said, "Hello, Michael." And Michael could hear it and quickly turned to his friends in the front seats. They were lost in their worlds of whatever entertainment they had to make the long drive go by quicker.

Michael turned back to the man in the other car. He didn't want to turn and look back because he was afraid that he would be sitting beside him. Michael was right; the man was sitting in their car now, smiling at Michael. "I said hello, Michael. Don't be rude," the man said. "I do believe you asked what a portal to hell looks like. Well, I'm just the fallen angel to show you." He laughed.

Michael was afraid, to say the least. He thought that he felt like a helpless child trying to go to bed, but the lights were off, and there may be a monster under his bed. As a child, he would run as quickly as he could and jump just before the monster got him.

The man beside him began to laugh and said, "You were right to jump. I was under your bed. I could have grabbed you, but I enjoyed your fear. I feasted on your fear for many years. That's not why I'm here. You asked about a portal. I'm going to show you, my good man. Don't worry, I'm not going to try to buy your soul. There are plenty of dumb people who are lining up to give me their souls. I personally like watching you do battle with the forces of evil. Pretty exciting, my man. The good thing is that you die in the end." He began to laugh again. "All of you talking monkeys die. So here we go. I want you to tell me what you've learned after the story."

Michael's glasses went dark as he could still hear the man say, "Enjoy."

Michael could see two people driving an old pickup truck down a two-lane highway. The couple was Chris and Kelly from northern Iowa. They had been together since high school. When Chris dropped out, Kelly soon followed. Chris thought of himself as an outlaw. He was obsessed with the tales of Bonnie and Clyde. Bonnie and Clyde had it wrong, though, because they got ambushed. That was not going to happen to Chris and Kelly. Chris had a system that had not gotten them caught yet. They would scope out a place, drive to the next town, steal a car, and drive back to the first town. Chris would rob the place—the last one was a gas station—and Kelly would be the wheelman.

"I heard these famers out here don't like banks. I say we stay on one of these guys' farms for a minute. We help them out with work and see if they got some money. If they don't, we move on. But if they do, we use that to get one day closer to Vegas."

Kelly agreed with Chris. He pulled off the main road and saw a back road. This back road led to a house that was close to the highway. Chris thought that this was perfect. If "the man" showed up, they could burn out on the highway and get away. They pulled up to the main house and saw a man working in the garden with his wife. "Hello there, sir," Chris said.

"Hello, young people. How can we help you?" the old man said.

"Well, my name is Chris, and this is my lady, Kelly. We are on our way to the coast, and we are looking to work our way there. I'm from Iowa and know my way around a farm. If you don't have any money, that's cool. We are looking to get off the road for a while. I can mend a fence and fix a roof. You name it, and I can probably do it," Chris said.

The old man looked at his wife, and she nodded. "Sounds good, son. You two are welcome to stay in the backhouse by the barn. Go ahead and get settled, and dinner will be at six." The old man shook Chris's hand.

Chris felt his grip and thought, This is a strong man.

The two got themselves together in the spare rooms. They cleaned up and headed to the main house for dinner. At dinner, Kelly saw what kind of people they were. They said grace and thanked God for Chris and Kelly. Kelly couldn't remember the last time she heard someone say a prayer for her and truly mean it. After dinner, Chris and Kelly lay in the dark. Kelly said, "Maybe we could just hang here for a while. I don't think they have any money. Even if they do, I don't want to."

"I got us this far. Just do what I say. These people are probably scumbags like all the others," Chris said.

The next day, the old man put Chris to work. They started by repairing the fence on the west side of the property. Kelly started working on the lady's car. She asked Kelly where she learned the skill. Kelly said that she learned from her uncle Joe. He showed her how to do oil changes and work on engines. She did that until she was about fifteen years old. That year, her uncle and Dad were killed by a drunk driver. Her mother passed away two years later from cancer. Chris came into her life and took care of her. The lady smiled at Kelly and gave her some ice tea.

The rest of the week was just the same. Chris would work in the fields or with the animals, and Kelly would help the lady. Chris got the old man talking about banks. He said that his grandfather never trusted banks. All bankers were there to steal honest people's money. The old man agreed with Chris. He told him that he had valuables hidden around. "I have a safe or two round my property. Then there is the most valuable thing besides a man's woman hidden. It's whatever man wants in his life. I got that in a place even I can't reach anymore. It's tucked away," the old man said. They both watched the creek as they drank a beer.

Kelly was helping the lady in the garden. "Ariel, how long have you been living here with Gabriel?" Kelly asked.

"Well, let's see . . . I lose track of time. This was my father's land. He left it for us to tend. I can't remember, sweetie, probably just after the flood," the lady said. "I like you. You're welcome to stay as long as you like. If you need time to get yourself right, please stay here."

Kelly thought long and hard about her offer. She didn't see these people as strangers anymore. They seemed like the grandparents she never knew.

That night as Kelly and Chris were cleaning up for dinner, Kelly wanted to talk Chris out of ripping these people off. "Chris, these are good people. I don't want to hurt them."

Chris was in the bathroom. "I told you, babe, we need this! I looked through their bills! They aren't behind on anything! That old man said he had valuables all over this property! I'm going to find them!" Chris shouted.

"I'm not going to let you hurt them," Kelly said as she started walking to the door. She grabbed the door handle, and everything went dark for her. Chris had hit her over the head with the butt of his revolver.

"I said no," Chris said as he stood over her body. He kicked her side and noticed that she didn't move. "Come on, get up." He checked her neck, and he was shocked. She had no pulse, and she stopped breathing. "Kelly . . . Kelly. No, you can't be."

Chris got up and paced around the room, trying to think. "They did this to me. They turned you against me. Well, they're going to pay. Sorry, Kelly, but if you chose them here, you would probably rat me out later. We had a good time," Chris said to Kelly's lifeless body. Chris packed up his stuff and left her in the room. He threw his bag into his truck and walked to the main house with his revolver in his pocket.

Chris walked into the door and saw the two older people sitting in their chairs, staring at him.

The old man said, "Hello, Chris. Where's Kelly?"

"Where's Kelly? Don't worry about Kelly. You need to worry about your own lady," Chris said as he pulled out his revolver. The couple showed no fear or surprise.

"I take it you want your money," the old man said as he pointed to a stack of bills lying on the table.

Chris took the money and said, "That's a good start, but I want all your stuff."

"OK, Chris, tell me what you want," the old man said.

"I want all your money, and I want you to tell me where that stuff is where you can't reach anymore!" Chris shouted.

"Are you sure, Chris?" he said.

"If you don't, I'm going to shoot your lady in the stomach, and you can watch her die slowly. Then I'm going to kill you the same way," Chris said.

"No need to threaten us with violence. I'll show you where," the old man said.

Chris pulled out a pair of handcuffs and told the old man to restrain his lady to the stairs. The old man did, and when Chris was certain that the old lady could not get away, they both set off across the field. The sun was still up, but the old man brought a flashlight and some rope.

They reached the far side of the field and passed through a gate. About twenty-five yards from the gate, they came onto an old well. "It's down there. In the place of a brick, I put a small safe in the wall off the well. I did that when I was young like you. The lock is broken. It doesn't lock. The well isn't deep. It's only about ten feet deep," the old man said.

Chris tied the old man with the rope against the closest tree. With the extra rope, he dropped it down the well. "Now if I feel you moving around to try to get free, I'm killing you. Then I'm killing that old bag too," Chris said as he lowered himself into the well. It was about ten feet deep.

Halfway to the bottom, Chris saw a metal box where a stone should be. He thought that this old man was a lot of things, but he wasn't a liar. Chris braced himself against the wall of the well and opened the metal door. He saw two gold bars sitting in the box. He picked one up, and it was heavy. Putting the light on it, he knew it was real. He then grabbed the other bar and cradled them in his arms. He looked in the box, and he was confused. The back of the box was lit up as if it was a door—a door with a bright light on the other side.

Chris reached into the box and pushed on its back. The back flew open like a door. He was blinded for a second, and then he was amazed. He saw Kelly and himself. They were standing at the movie theater where they met. In fact, it was the very moment they met. It was real; he could hear Kelly talking and smell the popcorn from the concession stand. He watched a younger him ask for Kelly's name. Kelly looked so beautiful and young. He called out to Kelly, and the box went dark.

Chris looked up, and the well was sealed close. He climbed up to the top, and it was sealed by a wooden door or metal plate. The well was bricked up with the same bricks as the walls. It looked as if it had been sealed a long time ago. Chris pushed on the top and screamed to let him out. He looked at the rope. It looked as if it was sandwiched between the rocks.

A light came from the box below him. Chris climbed down to see what the box was showing. As he climbed back down, the two gold bars fell to the bottom of the well. They hit the ground and sunk into the ground like seeds planting themselves. Chris looked into the box and saw Kelly. She was alive and working in the old people's farm. "Thanks for letting me stay here," Kelly said.

"It's our pleasure. We are happy to have you work off debt, and before you know it, you'll be on your way to your next life, sweetheart," the old woman said.

The box went dark again, and Chris felt something tugging on his shoe. Vines were growing from the well floor, and they were pulling at him. The ends of the vines had bird talons on them. They scratched and tore at Chris. The box then gave him one last image. He saw Kelly hugging the old people and thanking them. The old woman dropped the keys to the truck to Kelly. Kelly jumped into the truck and drove down the interstate. She disappeared over the horizon just as the sun rose over it. The old couple both turned and looked at Chris. "Welcome, Chris. That well is your home for a long time," the old man said. The box went dark, and the flashlight went out. Chris lost his footing and was pulled to the floor of the well, and the wood talons clawed at him.

The image went dark, and Michael could only hear Chris calling for help. Soon the cries for help faded away, and Michael could see the inside of the car he was riding in. "That was a good tale, don't you think?" the man said to Michael.

Michael just stared at him, wondering what he was going to do next.

"You see, Michael, people make their own hell. I just keep them happy with the choices they make. Now Kelly made some poor choices. She was lucky enough to get a second chance. She worked on that farm and paid back the debt she owed to life. You didn't see her working on that farm for years. She didn't complain one day. Kelly was rewarded for her hard work. The dog she had when she was a little girl came to the farm and stayed with her. When she lay down every night after work, her childhood pup would curl up beside her," the man said as he looked out the window.

A large red truck drove up behind their car and started tailgating them. The man became excited upon the truck's arrival. "Oh, how I love people who tailgate. I think I'm going to take a ride with this cowboy. You have a nice journey. I will be watching you with pleasure." The man smiled wide, almost cartoonish. The red truck drove speeding by. Michael could see the man appear in the passenger seat next to the driver. He put on the driver's cowboy hat and began to laugh at him. The man then held the driver's hat outside the window as if he was a cowboy on a bull.

Michael felt his lunch coming up. He quickly grabbed Craig by the arm and told him to pull over because he was going to puke. As soon as the car stopped, Michael jumped out and threw up behind the car. April and Craig raced to the back of the car to see if Michael was OK. "I'm good. I think I got a little motion sickness," Michael said on his knees. April gave Michael a bottle of water and sat back in the car.

Craig said, "OK, buddy, you hop in whenever you're ready." He walked to the front of the car and started talking on the phone. It looked as if he needed to stretch his legs too.

Soon the sickness passed, and Michael stood up. He looked across some field, and that was where he saw it. The farmhouse was right there. He saw the farmhouse that Chris and Kelly wandered into. Looking at the main house, he saw an old man working on a tractor. The old woman was working in her garden. Both people had their backs toward Michael. He looked at their fence line by a line of trees and tried to see the well. He looked back at the people who were still working. As Michael was staring at the people, they turned in unison and looked at Michael. They both waved at Michael as if he was an old friend. Michael waved back reluctantly.

The old man started pointing down toward the ground. He pointed at his eyes and then down toward the ground. Michael looked in front of him as if he was looking for something on the ground. He saw a stone about five feet from the road. It looked like the stones from his county park but the size of a dinner plate. Michael looked at his friends and noticed they were not paying attention to him. He walked over to the stone and lifted it. Under the stone was a black horn. It was old and had a handwriting on it. It was not hollow, but it was filled with a stonelike substance. The top was smooth. He thought he saw the symbol on one of the stones outside Mr. Blackfoot's cabin.

Michael placed the horn into his pocket and looked up at the man. The people and the farm were gone. Michael looked down at the stone, and it was gone too. He felt for the horn in his pocket, and it was still there. "I'm ready to go now. Maybe we could stop at the next gas station, please," Michael said to Craig. Craig nodded, and they both got into the car. They continued down the road. Michael tried to forget about the driver who was tailgating them, but the thought of him would not leave his mind.

Chapter 20

ROAD RAGE

Justin's large red truck drove down the highway. He was speeding down the highway like he always did. Justin's commute to work was a long one. He drove twenty-five minutes from his home in the next town over to work as a mechanic. Justin worked in three of the shops in his hometown. He was fired from all of them. The first one was because he was late all the time. The second one was because he was late all the time, and he complained about having to do "the crap" jobs. Of course, the last one was because he was late.

The last shop was owned by one of his friends' dad who was reluctant to hire him. His son told his dad that Justin was just misunderstood. Justin's boss had to let him go because he was unreliable. Justin didn't like this reason for termination, so he got into a pushing match with the owner. He didn't win the pushing match and didn't get his job back. Justin had to get a job in the next town. He would leave early at first, and then his old ways came back into play. When he was late, it was never his fault. He had car troubles, the drivers on the road were driving too slowly, or he drank too much the night before.

Driving down the road, Justin tailgated a car in front of him until he could pass. That stupid driver, he thought. He glared at the occupants inside as he sped past. Was it three or four people in the car? That confused him; he couldn't stop thinking about the number of people in the car until a chill went up his spine.

He quickly forgot about the people, and he thought, Forget those people. I'll drive as fast as I want to. It's your fault I'm late 'cause you drive like an old lady.

Justin got off the highway and pulled down the main road. Driving like he was in a race car movie, Justin pulled into the shop's lot. He walked into the shop like nothing was wrong. As soon as he timed in, his boss asked to see him. He slowly walked to the office. Justin had made that walk plenty of times. "Justin, this is the last time. I can't have you come in here late every day. This is the seventh time in two weeks. Before that, it was five times in two weeks. I got to let you go. Sorry," his boss said.

"This is bull. It's not my fault," Justin said. He then kicked over a chair and told his boss he'd be sorry. He stormed out of the shop unemployed yet again.

Justin sat in his car mad at the world but mostly at his former boss. He thought, I'll get him back today, right now. I know where he lives. He's got that '69 Pontiac GTO that he drives on the weekend. I'll park on the dollar store up the street and walk through the neighbor's property. I know I can hot-wire it. Justin drove his car to the dollar store parking lot; he pulled over by the neighbor's property. The property was wooded and had a fence line about ten feet from the lot. Justin saw a No Trespassing sign on the old fence. He decided that he was going to trespass and steal a car.

He slipped through an opening in the fence. On the other side of the fence, the property was thicker than he thought. He knew it was at least a football field worth of property to cross, but he didn't care. As he walked through the property, he noticed a Danger: Keep Away sign. Justin thought that the sign was redundant.

Some of the plants and foliage looked strange. He had worked for a landscaping company for a short time and had never seen some of these plants. Justin continued walking through the property and came to a small clearing. He could see the house. It was a run-down old house. It had an old green house on the west side of it. This part of the house was covered in vines and debris. He thought, Maybe I should turn back and walk around this place.

As soon as Justin thought that, the front door opened, and two massive dogs came out to do their business. Justin froze and slowly walked back into the woods. When he lost sight of the dogs, he heard them bark. The barks were far away at first, and then they got closer. Justin turned and ran as fast as he could. He ran blindly into the woods, not knowing if he was running back to the spot where he came in.

Justin stumbled into a small clearing the size of a kiddie pool. In the middle of the clearing was a mud pond. Justin sank about a foot into the pool. He thought, Oh my god, I'm in a quicksand. All my life, I thought I wouldn't find quicksand, and now here it is. Justin didn't keep sinking; he just stayed at the same level.

The dogs were the next thing he was thinking of. He thought, These dogs are going to find me and bite the hell out of me. I got to get out. Justin struggled to get out, and then he felt a sharp pain in the back of his neck. It felt like a long needle entering his skin. He swatted at his neck and felt a large bug. Looking around, he saw dozens of large red and orange bugs flying around him. The bugs looked flying scorpions with their tails turned in. A two-inch needle came out of the tails. The head looked like a red bumblebee. The wings on the bugs were beautiful. They reminded Justin of fairy wings, two on the top and two on the bottom.

He threw himself onto the ground and pulled himself from the mud. He thought, My feet aren't moving. My legs are going numb. The bug must have paralyzed me. I can crawl to my car. I hope these things won't follow me. Justin crawled toward what he hoped was the fence line. He looked back and saw that the bugs were not following him.

Crawling through the trees, he felt his legs getting heavier and heavier. He thought, You can make it, just a little further to the fence. Justin looked up and saw he had made it to the fence line. He pulled himself into the clearing between the trees and the fence line.

At this time, he felt numb from the waist down. He lay by the fence and looked down at his legs with horror. A cocoon had grown over his legs to just below his chest. The cocoon was gray and brown. It pulsated on different spots. He tried to scream, but he was exhausted. Justin tried to push it off with his left hand. The cocoon stuck to his hand like the mud he was in. It then pulled his hand into the cocoon. It started to grow faster up his body. He thought, This is it. I'm going to die in this gross ball. The cocoon had Justin up to his head. The back of his head was covered up and pulled into the rest of the cocoon.

Inside, Justin saw green slime. He thought, OK, I should die from lack of air, but I'm not. I can taste this stuff. It's gross like sticking my tongue on a battery. I feel funny. There's a light, and I can move.

Justin moved toward the light. He emerged from the cocoon and found himself on the ground. He thought, That stuff must still be in my eyes. Everything looks funny. It looks like everything is in panoramic view. Justin stood up, but it felt funny. He walked over to the fence, and he felt taller. He grabbed the fence and noticed that he could see far along the fence. He looked down at his body. It was gone, not gone—changed. He was one of those bugs.

His legs and body were replaced by six alien legs. He thought, Oh my god, I'm a bug. This can't be real! Oh my god! My car, I can get to my car . . . eat. He headed toward his car. It felt like he was walking, but he knew he was flying. The wind was pushing him hard.

He landed on the hood of his car. Justin was able see himself in the reflection of the windshield. He thought, I'm a bug. Eat. I should be freaking out, but I'm not . . . eat. Justin could figure out why he was thinking of eating. Eat was just popping into his head.

He was trying to figure out what when the wind blew him from his car. Justin had no control of where he was going. He felt like he was on a roller coaster with no straps. The wind stopped pushing him, and he could see down the road. He stayed there for a moment. He felt his humanity drifting away. What's my name? Jeff, Joey, something with a

J. Eat. I feel my thoughts and memories fading. Justin! Eat. Justin is my name. Eat. If I can just remember my name I can—

Justin's body exploded on the front of a semitruck headed northbound on the highway. The truck driver looked on his windshield and saw a little bug leg on the glass. He hit the wipers and cleaned it off. "That was a big one. I'll need to clean that off at the next stop," the truck driver said.

A chill went up the driver's spine. Sitting next to him was a man in a formal suit. His hair was black and slicked back with oil. The man in the suit smiled large and began to speak, knowing the truck driver couldn't see or hear him. "Sorry, Justin. Maybe the next time you tailgate someone, make sure the devil isn't a passenger," he said as he began to laugh hysterically.

<h1>Chapter 21</h1>

<h1>GARDEN WITCHES</h1>

The crew rolled through Kansas. They headed toward Michael's hometown to drop him off. Craig's phone went off, and he had news after the phone call. "We are headed to here," Craig said as he pointed to his phone's map. "We are headed to a site where they had witchcraft. Back in the '70s, a group of women started a cult. The house we're seeing is the ruins of it. One night in October, they had a fire that killed three of them. The city owns the property now. The local neighborhood watch plants flowers there and keeps it up. The local government keeps it in their hands. During Halloween, the firefighters park in front and hand out candy."

"Great witches," Michael said. He kept his glasses off until they reached the town.

They pulled up to the lot, and it was beautiful. The chimney was all that was left of the house. It was repaired and painted by locals. Flower beds surrounded the chimney. A picnic table was in the yard with a sealed box on top. The box read "Witch House Garden donation." Michael thought it was pretty neat. On the side of the chimney was a list of events that were going to happen. Someone had written in today's date and put "Scare Crew filming."

The crew set up their equipment. April and Craig went walking around the neighborhood, looking for people to talk to. After Michael set his stuff up, he sat at the picnic table and put on his glasses. He made sure to look down at his phone to make it look like he was browsing. "I don't want to see the women burn. Tell me of the dangers of this place now." The glasses went dark, and Michael heard a witch's cackle.

The glasses focused on the neighborhood to the south of the ruins. He flew over the houses like a bird. The houses were beautiful. The grass was mowed to the same height on every yard. The flower beds were amazing. The variety of flowers looked like a professional came and planted each one. He then saw that behind a row of houses was a creek. On the other side of the creek was normal-looking houses. Some were vacant; some had crappy cars, and the yards looked different.

Michael saw an Olds Cutlass parked on the side of the road. Two people had gotten out and walked through the tree line into the creek. They climbed up the banks of the creek to the other side. They crawled to the back edge of one of the houses. "This is the place. I was in the county with Jake. His girl said this lady has tons of stuff. She used to work for that maid's place. She broke a lamp downstairs, and the old lady never even heard it. I figure we go in through the back basement door. When we're done, we'll look in this shed," Nick said to Travis.

Both men walked up to the back door. Nick looked around the back and saw dozens of garden gnomes. For some reason, this spooked him. They were by the house, in flower beds, and by the birdbaths. The gnomes were doing different tasks—holding lamps, smoking pipes, pushing wheelbarrows, and doing other lawn activities. Nick blew it off and slowly opened the rear basement door. "If we hear dogs, we go," Nick said.

They walked in and saw a cat looking at them. Cats were OK as far as Nick was concerned. In the basement, there were two main rooms, one a large sitting area with couches and bookcases. The other main room was a large kitchen. Travis started putting stuff from the sitting room in his bag. Nick watched the cat disappear under the stairs and headed toward the kitchen. In the silverware drawers was actual silverware.

"This lady is loaded," Nick said to himself. He was finishing up when he heard a large thump. It sounded like Travis fell.

He went to see and saw him on the floor. Nick went over to see him. "What's wrong, man?" Nick whispered to him. Travis looked up in terror at Nick, totally paralyzed. A thin porcupine-like needle was in the side his neck.

"What the . . ." Nick said as a sharp pain hit his throat. He looked at the stairs and saw a little old lady smiling at him. Her cat was rubbing against her legs. Nick fell to the floor, and everything went dark.

"It's OK, my sweet," Nick heard the old woman say. His eyes were blurry at first, but then he saw the old woman. She was standing over Travis, who was hog-tied. "Well, look who's awake. Hello, sonny. I see you two entered my house without my permission." Travis was tied up and had a plastic bag covering his body. Nick looked at his body, and he was tied up in a trash bag. His head was the only thing sticking out. He tried to yell, but he was gagged.

The old lady looked like she was in her nineties and weighed under 100 lbs. "I was fair, Nicholas. I flipped this coin. Travis won the honor of being the guest of honor tonight. You will be helping me with my lawn. That will be in my 'she shed.' Let's get to work. Don't worry 'bout your car. I'll have the police tow it." The old lady cackled.

She walked over to Travis, who was lying by a large metal oval. The oval had holes in it like a spaghetti strainer. She picked up Travis with no effort at all. Travis weigh about 250 lbs. She lifted him like a loaf of bread. Travis gave a muffled scream as she sealed him into the metal oval. She then picked up the giant dishwater and walked it over to a cabinet door. The old lady opened the door, and Nick saw a hot-tub-sized pot with boiling water. Above the pot was a cover. The old woman slid Travis into the pot and pulled down the lid. She closed the cabinet door and said, "He'll cook for six hours. I'll add the veggies later."

The lady picked up Nick and put him in a wheelbarrow. She pushed his head into the bag and wheeled him outside. Nick tried to get free, but he couldn't. "I need to open the shed doors, my sweet," she said with a cackle. Nick was tipped over to the floor. The bag opened up, and he was in the middle of the floor. He saw the old lady, and her appearance had changed. Her hair was long, gray, and oily. Her skin was a light green, and her nose was long and crooked, like a root from the ground. She smiled with her yellow teeth.

The old witch dug her long bony fingers into a bucket of mud. She began to smear the mud all over Nick's body. He was frozen with fear. As she did, she began to chant Latin. Nick couldn't believe this was happening. She shoved two bamboo straws in his nose. The old witch then held his mouth closed. Nick saw her hold a long crescent needle with red thread. She held his mouth closed and started to sew his mouth shut. Her chanting became louder and faster. When she was done sewing, she smeared mud over his head, mouth, and face. Nick closed his eyes and struggled to breathe from his bamboo nose straws. He could hear the old witch chanting when the mud started to harden. He couldn't scream, but he wanted to. The last thing he heard was the old witch saying, "I think you'll look good in blue."

That night, the old lady's house was full of old women. They had a feast with plenty of leftovers. Days passed, and the old lady's yard looked more beautiful than it had. The flowers looked brighter, and the lawn looked full. A sign on the yard said, "Yard of the month." That sign came with a $25 gift card to the local hardware store. By the bay window was a new garden gnome. The gnome was a foot tall, and he was sitting with his legs crossed. He had a bright blue jacket and a blue hat. On the hat was painted the name "Nick." As Michael watched the gnome sit there, he could hear a muffled scream from its mouth.

The glasses went dark, and then the picnic table came back to view. Michael looked across the lot to the houses. He could see the yards.

All the yards had gnomes in them. It looked as if the gnomes had a convention. He stood up and walked to the edge of the street, trying not to but counting the gnomes. "Are you from Hollywood, young man?" an old lady said behind him.

Michael turned and saw the old lady from the glasses' story. "I'm with the show, ma'am," he said.

"Thank you for coming tonight. I hope this will bring more visitors to our community," she said as she slowly walked by him.

Michael stood still as she walked by. He thought, Take off your glasses. You're about to see something you don't want to.

With her back to Michael, she said, "Have a beautiful night . . . Michael." The old lady looked back over her shoulder with a sinister grin. Michael could instantly see her true form—the green skin and dirty, oily hair.

"My god, she knows my name," he said under his breath. As the old lady slowly walked away, she gave Michael a soft cackle.

That night, Michael was never alone. They did their show, and Michael asked to go home. He would meet up with them in a few days after they dropped him off. He realized that he needed a break.

Chapter 22

LOUISE

Michael got out of the car as they stopped for gas. He stretched his legs and walked into the gas station. After using the bathroom and getting a drink, Michael walked back to the car. He looked down the street and saw a man cutting the lawn. Michael didn't know why this man caught his eye. When Craig was about to pull off, Michael asked if they would drive down that street where he saw the man. Craig drove slowly down the road, and Michael put on his glasses. With his glasses on, Michael saw the man sitting on the front steps, drinking some water. The man was taking a break from lawn care. Two elderly people were working in the garden. They seemed happy. The lady sat back on her knees and took a drag off a beer. Michael looked over his glasses, and they were gone. He assumed that these were spirits.

Michael looked back through the glasses and asked Craig to pull over for a second. They stopped and started texting. Michael watched the man on the steps answer his phone and get up. He pushed his lawn mower into the back and jump into his car. The two old people stopped digging in the garden. The old man stood up and helped his lady up. She stood up with her beer in hand and gave it to her man. The old man slammed the rest of the beer, and they walked to the car. Michael looked back to the man in the car, and the old couple was already sitting in back. The old man had his arm around his lady. The man backed up and pulled away. It was clear that he didn't see them. As they drove by, the

"""

old couple waved at Michael, clearly seeing that he saw them. Michael smiled and waved back.

"OK, man, I'm ready," Michael said. They pulled off and headed back to Michael's hometown. Michael asked the glasses to show him that couple's story. The glasses went dark, and then he saw the woman, younger, lying in bed, watching TV.

Louise lay in bed, watching TV. She was tired and wanted to fall asleep, but she was afraid. She was afraid he was coming back. It was not her husband or a boyfriend she was afraid of; it was a creature.

Louise was a mother of four and happily married. Her husband, Ed, is a good man. He worked at a factory and supported his family. Recently, he got a change of schedule at his job. They talked about the change and what it meant for their family, an extra ten thousand dollars a year and room for growth. The downside was that he'd be working nights. Nights are miserable for people who actually like being around each other.

The kids went to school in the morning as Dad walked in from work. A quick kiss between them, and Dad went to bed. Louise went to work and left her hubby to sleep. When she got home, the kids were finishing up their homework. After she made dinner, Dad ate quickly and headed off to work. The kids got louder as the night went on. The threat of "calling your father" came out, and quiet was restored. She put the kids to bed and had a glass of wine. That was her normal for a while. She would go to sleep alone.

The first couple of nights was OK. That big bed was all to herself. A few nights into it, she missed the hubby. One night she woke up out of the blue. She lay there and looked across the bedroom. On the door hung her robe, the Mother's Day robe she got last year. The robe hung on the door about a foot taller than her. She looked at it and knew it was her robe because she put it there. In the dark, it did not look like a robe. She remembered as a child the things in her room would change after the lights went out. The pile of clothes would turn into an evil troll. The coats hanging up would be ghostlike black creatures. The dolls sitting across from her looked back at her with wide unblinking eyes. This memory entered and stayed in her mind. The robe looked as if it were a man hunched over against the door. He glared at it as she lay in her bed. She thought, I saw too many scary movies when I was a kid.

Louise tried to go back to sleep when a thought was thrust into her mind. It was as if someone or something opened her mind and rammed this image in. Her mind began to remember a specific time as a young girl, a time when she had her own room and didn't have to share with her elder sister. In this memory, she remembered a man or manlike creature walking outside her window. It felt like a nightmare at the time. Every time she turned on a light, the creature would leave. She didn't want to act like a baby, so she would turn it off. This happened many times. She never got a good look at him. She only saw glimpses of him. The thing she remembered most was his skin. It was scaled like a snake. She would call him the Snake Man. These encounters happened for a few weeks until the family dog started sleeping in the room.

Louise kept thinking about the encounters as a child. The robe looked like a man hunched over, but it slowly began to come into view. The streetlights bled into the room and on the robe figure. She thought her imagination was playing tricks on her. The figure slowly started to develop snakelike scales. She turned the light on, and it turned back into a robe.

The next couple of nights, she turned on the TV, and the figure disappeared. The thought of taking down the robe came in, but then she thought it would mean she truly believed in the Snake Man. She would lie in her bed and think. She would think about everything—missing her husband, missing her sister, and thinking about her kids. They lived with her now, but before she knew it, they would leave. They would leave for school or a job. That was a good thing. She wanted them to have their own lives. A piece of their parents would be with them always. It just hurt when a baby you devoted your whole self to went into a cold, unforgiving world. Gone were the days when the boys would come into the room at night because of a nightmare. "Mom, can I sleep with you?" had changed to "I'm not a baby anymore." The daily feedings had changed to the boys eating as fast as they can so they can get back to their own worlds.

Louise got up to look out the window. With only the TV on, she could see outside very easily. Their bedroom had a view that showed the street in front of the house. Across from the house were some woods. Louise looked into the woods that were illuminated by the streetlight. She knew her eyes may be playing tricks on her, but she stood focused on a small part of the woods. A tree, she thought, about half the thickness of a light pole caught her eye. The tree slowly turned into that familiar figure. The longer she stared, the more she could see the long scaled arms. It stood at least seven foot tall. She looked where the face would be, and a pair of eyes started to glow. Looking at the eyes, Louise started to hear a voice in her head. I'm here, Louise. I've always been here. Your boys can't help you forever. Louise closed the curtains and jumped into bed.

The next day, she told Ed that they needed to talk when he got up. Ed got up an hour early to speak with her. She told him that she didn't care about the money, and she wanted him home. Ed agreed with her, and he said he'd put in for a transfer back to his original shift. That night, Louise slept with the TV and lights on. The weekend came with a good surprise. Ed said he was going back to day shift, and they would not lose any salary.

Life continued for the family. Ed started his normal hours, and the Snake Man didn't return. The boys grew with time. The oldest boy went off to college and started a family a few years later. He moved across town and then across the country. The second and third boys went into the services. They lived their lives seeing the world and serving their country. They both came back home and started their own families. The last to leave went into law enforcement. He stayed in his community he grew up in and started his own family. Louise's house went from loud to quiet. Grandkids came and brightened their lives.

When it came to the end, Louise fell asleep on her couch. She woke up, and Ed had gone to bed. He had cut the grass, and that wore him out. On her couch, the lights were off, and just the TV was on. She turned the TV off to go to bed. Once the TV was off, the room was in total darkness. She thought, Maybe I should have turned a light on first. She didn't want to fall like she did a couple of years ago. Louise went to turn the TV back on, but nothing happened. A light from under the closet door shone and slightly illuminated the room.

Standing in front of her was the Snake Man. He stood tall in front of the old woman. He was as young and strong as the time she thought she saw him. The figure became clear. His scales covered his whole body. Long arms and legs came out of this thin body. His eyes glowed with hate toward her. "I told you I'd come back. I always wanted you. Your boys have left you, and your husband is too old to save you from me," the Snake Man said.

"Why do you want me?" Louise said.

"Because you love. You taught your boys to love. They are teaching their kids to love. I hate love. This is my time to strike. You die this night. You're here until you're ready. You'll never be ready. I'll rip you apart till there's nothing left, and no one can stop me," the Snake Man said as he closed in.

She sat in fear, thinking she was a helpless old lady alone. Louise stopped thinking of the Snake Man, and she didn't feel alone. She stood up, and the Snake Man took two steps back. Racing through her mind were feeding her kids at breakfast; watching her boys play sports; drive-in theaters with her hubby; trick-or-treating with the kids, first her boys and then her grandkids; and driving in the car to California for vacation.

The Snake Man fell to his knees before her. "I'll leave. I won't bother your family. Just let me go," he said.

Louise looked at him, confused, because he was looking all around her. She looked to the right and left of her and saw her boys. They were standing beside her. At first, they were boys, and then they changed into the men she knew they were. On her shoulders, she felt two hands. She knew those strong hands. Those were the hands of the man who would help her build her family. Her men looked at her and then asked, "Mom?"

Louise smiled and said, "Go ahead, boys."

The men tore the Snake Man apart. Louise looked at her men and said, "Oh no. If I'm dead, that means you're all dead too."

Ed smiled at her and said, "No, sweetheart. We're still alive. What you see now is the part of your boys' souls that they gave you and mine. When you're ready, we'll move on together."

Louise smiled and cried as she began to see her parents, brothers, sisters, friends, and grandchildren appear. She stood up and said, "Let's go."

Louise grabbed her daddy's hand. "I missed you, Daddy," she said with tears.

"I know, mija. Ready?"

She nodded, and they walked outside into the sunrise.

Michael took his glasses off and began to cry. The man he saw cutting the grass was her youngest son. Seeing both parents together made Michael believe that Ed could have died, but he thought, alive or dead, they would be with all their kids. He started thinking of the brothers story he saw earlier. He looked outside the car window, thinking. He hoped that these stories were true. Everyone you love gives you a piece of their souls. That piece is always with you. It protects you, keeps you from being lonely, and stays with you in every life you have.

Michael put in his earpieces for his phone and began to listen to a song by Warrant.

Got a picture of your house, and you're standing by the door;

It's black and white and faded, and it's looking pretty worn.

I see the factory that I worked silhouetted in the back;

The memories are gray, but man, they're really coming back.

I don't need to be the king of the world

As long as I'm the hero of this little girl;

Heaven isn't too far away,

Closer to it every day

No matter what your friends might say.

Chapter 23

Home Again

The crew dropped Michael off at his house. He checked his mail and grabbed his keys. He headed off to the store. He bought some stuff for the fridge and a lot of salt. When he got back, he put his food away and grabbed the salt. Michael read on the internet that salt and witches don't get along. He poured the salt around his house like the bug guy did when he sprayed his house. When he was done, Michael called his boy and then had a beer. He watched TV for a while, and then he decided to call Mr. Blackfoot.

Mr. Blackfoot was happy to hear from him. They decided to meet up at the cabin by the county park. Mr. Blackfoot told Michael that his son took over as caretaker. He came around less, but he came around. Michael hadn't slept in his bed in a long time. He slept with the lights on.

The next day, Michael headed out to see Mr. Blackfoot. Michael arrived at the cabin with Mr. Blackfoot sitting outside. "Hello, Michael," the old man said.

"Hey, do I have some stories for you." Michael laughed. Both men went inside and talked. Michael told him about his journeys. Mr. Blackfoot had his son listen in on their visit. "Now can you tell me about this horn?" Michael asked.

Mr. Blackfoot looked at the horn and the symbols on it. He told his son to get the book. "The book?" Michael questioned.

"Yes, we have had oral legends passed from keeper to keeper. During the 1800s, a smart man started writing them down. This is a copy of a copy of the original. The original is tucked away somewhere. This one is more durable," Mr. Blackfoot said.

"OK, the symbol on the top of the horn is fire. The symbol on the side is the cutting horn," the former caretaker said as he turned pages. "The cutting horn is a weapon given by the sky people. This weapon was given back to the sky people after a great battle with the eaters of men. This is a great blessing and curse. It's good that you have it, but it also means that the eaters of men will be in your path." Mr. Blackfoot was saddened.

"Thanks. How does it work?" Michael asked him.

"You will know when it's time," he said.

Michael thanked Mr. Blackfoot, and they talked a while longer. Mr. Blackfoot's son offered his help to Michael and asked him to call him whenever he needed him.

After his visit with Mr. Blackfoot Michael walked outside and asked the glasses, "How does the horn work?" The glasses flashed to E. Charles Grant's home. Michael was confused because that was the only image that he got. He decided to drive over to the residence. Michael hoped that he would not see that crazy man there. He killed him the last time they met—well, his mannequin killed him. The image of that night was replaying in his mind, a crazy man with a mannequin's face trying to kill him.

Michael pulled up to the house with some relief. It was completely gone. A barren spot where the basement was filled in remained. Michael still didn't understand why the glasses showed him the house. The house was gone, or was it?

Michael got out of his car and walked to the walkway. In the corner of his eye, he saw a glimmer. He turned to look at the glimmer, and it looked as if a star was shining of the ground. The light came from between the sidewalk and the grass. Michael bent over to look at the object and was shocked. It was the masher, the big marble that was flung into the mannequin's opening where his face was. The fire must have melted the mannequin, and the marble found itself out here. Michael grabbed the masher and put it in his pocket. He instantly felt better about everything. He was happy and energetic, and the images of his latest journey left him.

Michael walked up to the vacant lot where the house was. He thought of the fight for his life he had at this house. Michael wandered around the lot, looking at the discolored grass and bare spots. He stood looking at the backyard. There were a small tree and an old shed. He was about to walk away when the ground sunk in, and he fell to the bottom of what was the basement of the house. The hole was about five feet in diameter, and he fell about ten feet. Michael wasn't hurt when he landed. He looked around and saw most of the basement had been filled in. Something had hollowed out the basement to where he was sitting. He looked across from where he was sitting and thought he could see a tunnel.

Michael put his glasses on and asked to see clearly. The glasses changed, and he could see everything. He saw a tunnel and what was left of the basement. He could see it as if it was daytime in the tunnel. Michael moved his hands over the rocks and saw that he did not cast a shadow over them. Looking down the tunnel, he was amazed. The tunnel was about eight feet tall and five feet wide. "Whatever bore this out was big," he said to himself.

Michael started down the tunnel and felt his leg warm up. He reached into his pocket and pulled out the horn. It was warm but not hot. He held it up, and the letters on the side started to glow bright. On the top of the horn, the symbol started to glow red. Out of the top, a blade slowly started to come out like a switchblade. The blade grew to an arm's length and stopped. It glowed red as if it was pulled out of a forge. The steel had symbols on the side that looked like the horn. Michael looked over his glasses to see if the blade was glowing. He could see nothing but darkness. "I guess I got a weapon now. I wonder if I'll be able to tell the story about this," Michael said to himself.

He walked down the tunnel, looking at the sides and floor. They were dirt with rocks inside. At certain places, he saw claw marks on the sides. This gave Michael the chills. He walked a long way down the tunnel. It had a slight grade and had sharp turns every so often. Michael kept walking and thought if he came to a fork in the road, he would turn back. As he kept walking, he thought, I guess I could ask the glasses to show me the fastest way out of here. If I lose the glasses, I'm dead anyway.

Michael kept walking, thinking to himself and answering himself every so often. He came to an opening and slowly looked in. It was a cavern the size of a school basketball gym but oval. There was an opening at the top with a small amount of light and water coming down. Along the sides were three other openings. Michael looked at it without his glasses and saw nothing. He couldn't even see the little light from the top. In the center of the cavern was a stone slab. The slab looked like an old altar, but the groves on the slab looked fresh.

He heard someone coming and backed up. Michael hid behind a stone that was in front of the tunnel he came down from. He noticed that all the opening had a stone in front of them with different symbols.

Michael looked at the tunnel where the noise was coming from, and horror washed over him. He saw the driders carrying a bound man. The driders were too large to walk side by side down the tunnel. The first drider held the man up with his human arms. The bound man was hanging by his wrist from the giant man-spider. Once the creature came out of the tunnel, two more driders followed it. One of the driders grabbed the man by the legs and then walked to the stone altar.

The last creature was different. It was larger than the other ones and had a red cloth draped over its shoulders like a college graduate. Michael could see the bigger creature holding a sack in its arms. The sack looked like a huge spider egg sack. It pulsated in the monster's arms. The driders put the man on the stone slab and stretched him out.

Michael thought, I can't let this go on. He started toward the back of the closest creature as quick as he could. He raised the sword and brought it down between its bloated abdomen and body. The sword cut through the drider as if it was not there. The creature let out a bloodcurdling scream as Michael gave a follow-up swing to the right side of its legs. The man's legs were free from the mortally wounded drider.

The two other driders looked at Michael. Michael held his weapon toward the remaining creatures and shouted, "Let him go!" The creature holding the top part of the man raised his free hand and brought it down on the man's head. Instantly, the man's head was smashed like an old pumpkin left over from Halloween.

The smaller drider crawled over the man toward Michael, who backed up for more room to maneuver. The drider reached his human hands down by its waist and slowly brought it up. Michael could see that it put metal gloves on its hands. The metal gauntlets had spikes on the knuckles, and its fingertips were triangle blades. Michael asked the glasses, "What should I do?"

A few seconds later, Michael said to himself, "Really, man, you suck." But he directed it to the glasses.

The drider stood up on its four back legs with its other limbs spread out, like a hug was going to come. Michael screamed and ran straight into the drider's body with his sword up. He sliced the creature in half as he reached the other side. Michael was covered in green goo. He looked at the last drider and pointed his sword at him. Michael could hear the creature laughing at him. "I thought I'd see you, Michael. You win this time, but next time, it won't be so easy. This town is yours again. Keep it. We won't be back here. Soon we will have our homeland." The drider raised and came down with all its force on the stone altar. Michael took some steps back as the stone altar fell into a cavern below. The drider jumped into the hole and was gone.

Michael looked down the hole and saw another cavern about a hundred feet deep. "I'm not chasing you," he said to himself.

Michael looked around the cave for any more danger. On the wall of the cavern was a small iron door. He walked over to it and saw it had writing on it. He felt as if he needed to help someone or something. Raising his sword, the lock began to glow as if it was where he needed to cut. He stuck his blade into the lock, and it opened. The door opened, and a little man was lying inside. He was the size of a child's doll. For a second, Michael thought of Patrick. This little man was half Patrick's size. The clothes and shoes were like Patrick's.

The little man moved and turned to look at Michael with fear. "It's OK, buddy. Are you OK?" Michael said to the little man.

"Are the spiders gone?" the little man said.

"Yup, can I help you?" Michael asked.

"My name is Scotty, and I'm in your debt." The little man jumped out of the holding cell onto Michael's shoulder. Michael was not afraid of the little guy. He felt as if he had known this little man his whole life.

"Let's get out of here so you can go home," Michael said to him.

"I don't have a home anymore. They destroyed it and killed my family," Scotty said.

"Well, you can stay with me, buddy," Michael said to him. He walked back to his tunnel with his new friend to head back home. Michael reached the surface and walked to his car. He opened the trunk and pulled out some rags to clean the green goo off him. Scotty wiped the green goo off his boots.

Michael gave him some water that was sitting in his car. "I could go for something to eat," Scotty said. Michael nodded as he turned his car on. He drove home wondering if this newfound friend was safe with him.

Chapter 24

REUNION

Michael brought Scotty home and asked him what he wanted to eat. Scotty laughed and said, "Whatever you got and a beer." Michael smiled and fixed dinner for both of them. He fixed some books for Scotty to sit on and had a TV tray for him. He watched as the little man ate as if he hadn't eaten in days. They ate dinner and watched the sports recaps. Michael asked Scotty about himself.

"Well, I'm over five hundred years old. I won't say how far. I used to live in the wood with my family until some big spiders came and killed my family. They imprisoned me for my luck. I have special gifts like your glasses and horn. Truly, thank you for saving me," Scotty said as he took a long drink. "I am that voice that tells you, 'Go ahead,' 'Look down,' or 'That team is going to win.' They were growing more spider guys to split me up. Kind of gross, huh?"

Michael thought, Does Patrick know Scotty? He asked the glasses.

Michael looked over to where the door normally appeared, and it instantly was there. The door flung open quickly, and Patrick ran out. "Scotty!" Patrick cried. Both men locked eyes and ran to each other. Patrick was twice as big as Scotty, and it showed when the hugged. "I thought you were dead."

"I was taken prisoner. My girls are dead. This guy killed two of the spider guys and saved my life. I owe him a life debt."

Patrick smiled and said, "Your girls are alive. They made it back to our realm. They broke a star to get away."

Scotty's face changed to happiness. "Thank god," he said.

"You don't owe me anything, Scotty. Go back with Patrick and your family," Michael said.

"It doesn't work that way, sport. I owe you. I'll go with him for a while, but our destinies are bound."

Patrick looked at Michael and smiled. "Thank you for saving my friend. We have been watching your boy, protecting him from things that want to harm you. He is the safest person you know. You will be tested again. The driders are trying to reclaim their homeland. This war will be your war. For your heroism and saving this man, I give you this ring." Patrick handed Michael a golden coin ring. "This ring, like your sword, will protect you. It turns into shield when you do battle. Go to your next site with your friends. Keep the ring and horn with you always."

Michael thanked Patrick and watched both men walk to the door. Scotty said, "I'll see you up north when you arrive." Both men entered the door, and then the door disappeared. Michael cleaned up and went to bed.

The next morning, Michael packed his stuff and headed to the airport. He left his car at his house and took a cab. On his ride to the airport, he thought about his son. Jacob was safe and had always been. This made him happy and ready for his next task. He looked on the cabdriver's dash and saw a gnome smiling at him. This sent a chill down his spine. He could still hear the cackle of the old witch in his mind.

The plane ride went without anything going wrong. The plane wasn't struck by lightning, and a monster didn't try to eat him. Michael landed, and he texted Craig that he arrived. After he deplaned, he looked around for his friends. Michael saw a new friend waiting for him. On top of the arrival sign was Scotty holding a sign that said "Mike." Michael smiled and waved. Scotty jumped off the sign and bounced onto Michael's shoulder. "How was your flight? Did you see a banshee?" Scotty said.

Michael said, "Maybe I should have left you for the driders." And then he laughed.

"It's all fun and games until you bring up those damn driders."

Michael apologized, and they headed to get his bags. An hour later, Craig and the rest of the crew showed up. "How was your home visit?" Craig asked.

"Good. I took care of a spider problem at home, so I'm ready to get back to work," Michael said.

Scotty said to Michael in his mind, So if you talk to me through your thoughts, I can hear you. This will keep you out of the crazy house.

Michael thought back, Good. Don't be reading my mind though.

They got into the back of the car, and they left. In the car, Michael told Scotty, So now what?

Scotty replied, Now you're not alone in your fight. Now we make some memories.

The crew traveled down the road to their next adventure, hopefully not their last.